Fresh off the
Starship

by
Ann Crawford

For permission to quote brief passages, please contact
info@lightscapespublishing.com.

ISBN 978-1-948543-82-8
CIP data will be available.

Dedicated to

Ashanta

&

Grace

CHAPTER 1

"Look—she's wakin' up!"

"Oh my goodness—could this be happening at last? Missy, sweetheart, are you really finally wakin' up?"

"Darlin', can you hear me?"

"Missy Girl, you comin' back to us?"

OMG—oh my galaxy...what a strange-sounding language! It seems to be all k's intermingled with whooshes of sssss and sshhhhh sounds! Is that English? I've studied English for eons, but it seems so different up close.

"She moved her hand again!"

"She's movin' her eyelids! Oh, Missy, are you actually wakin' up?"

The woman in the bed slowly opens her eyes and then quickly shuts them against the bright lights.

"Missy!" An older female human be-thing's voice cracks.

She opens her eyes again. The three people standing around and over her are blurry against the overhead light and the glare from the window. She counts two male humans and the female. She quickly shuts her eyes again.

Oh, that hurts! It hurts here.

"Missy, honey, can you hear me? Are you comin' back to us?" The older woman's voice breaks into a strange wailing noise.

"Darling girl, we thought we lost you," the older man says as her eyes flutter open again. "But yer comin' back to us, aren't you?"

"Missy," the younger man says, his voice breaking.

"Get the doctor!" the older man says.

The younger man rushes out of the room.

Her eyes slowly open even as she squints, trying to adjust to the bright light. *Wow, that starshine is radiant—even more than the one at home!*

A voice booms over the loudspeaker outside the room: "Dr. Livingston, please go to room two-fourteen. Dr. Livingston, please go to room two-fourteen, stat." Those words are immediately followed by, "Code blue, room two-eleven. Code blue, room two-eleven."

Ohhhhhhhh—what a strange place this is! Loud noises, awful smells, strange beings looking at me.

The woman struggles to lift her hand just a few inches off the bed, clearly shocked to see it. *Oh. Right. I'm one of those strange beings now.*

A woman in a white coat hurries into the room and looks over the machines next to the bed and hooked up to the woman in the bed.

"Yer a lucky lady," states the woman in white. "We almost lost you. In fact, we did lose you. But welcome back." She looks at the small family gathered in the room. "Yer one lucky bunch."

"Thanks, Dr. Livingston," the older man says through glistening eyes, "fer everything you've done."

Doctor. Doctor. There are so many definitions in that word. Why can't I remember anything? Where'd all my training go?

The woman in the bed just stares up at the group staring down at her.

This is odd. Do humans just stare at each other?

"Missy, how are you feelin'?"

She doesn't respond; she just looks at the younger man who asked the question. He looks at the doctor, who then addresses her. "Missy, can you say something to us? Anything at all?"

The woman starts to speak, but then stops. The sensations in her throat feel very unusual.

"Well, you've had a very, very long journey back here," the doctor says, reassuringly.

You're not kidding.

"We should give you some time," the doctor continues. She ushers the family out of the room.

When can I go back in the other direction?

The young woman can still see and overhear them talking in the hallway.

"Is she gonna be okay?" the older woman asks.

"How's her mind gonna be?" the older man asks.

"Well, we don't know yet," the doctor responds. "We have to give it some time. That was a horrific accident, and we're just lucky she didn't die. In fact, she did die fer a minute there, as you well know. I'm amazed she came back. She certainly wanted to be here, that's fer sure."

The older woman holds her hand to her mouth, pushing back a gasp. The older man puts his arm around her.

The group starts to walk back into the room.

"Don't push her," the doctor emphasizes. "Give her lots of time and space—she needs that."

Time and space. Oh, you have no idea.

"Missy," the young man says, his eyes looking strangely wet, like the older man's and woman's had been, "we've been with you the whole time you was here."

Isn't it supposed to be were *here?*

"One of us was always with you, takin' turns, the whole three months."

"Where am I?" she asks.

The group of three, obviously ecstatic that she can talk but dismayed by her question, turns to the doctor, who's still standing by the doorway, writing notes. She rushes in.

"Missy, yer in a hospital room. You had a terrible accident a few months ago, and we thought we lost you at one point. But yer a tough survivor and fought yer way back here."

That's truer than you know.

"Do you know yer name?"

The woman thinks for a minute and then shakes her head.

9

The young man takes her hand. "Yer Missy. Yer my Missy Miss."

She looks at him as if trying to recollect where in the world she would know him from. After a minute or so, she shuts her eyes.

"Perhaps we should just let her sleep some more," the doctor tells them. "That's when most of the body's healing takes place." She ushers them out of the room again. "Amnesia can be a strange, strange thing," the doctor starts to say. "The brain—" But she shuts the door and the voices are muffled.

Ohhhhhhh, I have a feeling I'm not in the Andromeda galaxy anymore.

She awakens to find the fabric by her bed had been pulled back, and there's an old female human be-thing in the bed next to hers.

"Nurse, how much longer 'til I can leave?" the elder asks.

"Oh, any day now. We just want to make sure yer up to snuff." The nurse checks the machines next to the old humanoid, but when she sees that the younger woman is awake—and staring—she smiles and then gently pulls the fabric back to block her view.

Snuff?

Later that night, the woman opens her eyes again to find the younger man in the chair by the bed. His eyes are shut while very strange noises come from his open mouth as he breathes.

His light hair—*that's what they refer to as hair, right?*—frames his face, while more light hair surrounds his mouth and covers his chin.

He's definitely quite nice to look at—for a humanoid. Well, I guess that's what I am now, too.

She looks around the room. *Where are all the spectacular colors of Earth?* The only splash of color is from the beautiful flowers that maybe the man had brought with him. The rest of the room seems to be white on gray on white on gray. The machines are at least shiny with flashing lights and have fun, familiar beeping sounds. Everything else is white. And gray. And some more white over there. With more gray.

The star isn't shining into the room—the planet must've turned away from it as it does—but she remembers a quick glimpse of the outside as the star was setting and just seeing more variations of white on gray on white on gray outside, too. Oh, perhaps the celestial ceiling was blue. And the star setting had cast glorious pinks and oranges on the white, fluffy gatherings of crystalized droplets. *What are those called? Oh, that's right...clouds. Oh my universe—what happened to all the knowledge I gained after studying for so long?*

She stares at her hands—front and back, front and back. She slowly lifts her arm and moves it back and forth in front of her, as if she's pushing it through...*Oh, what's that interesting word Earthbeings might call it? Oh, right...sludge.* "Oh! No wonder you beings are so grumpy!" she says aloud, to her own surprise.

The young man startles awake. "Missy? You talkin' to me?"

Missy starts to speak again but then touches her throat. "Very...dry."

He grabs the cup on her bedside table, but it's empty. "I'll go get you some water."

As soon he leaves, Missy addresses the air. "Is anyone there?" She pauses for a few seconds. "Can anyone hear me? Something went terribly wrong!"

"I'm here," comes the old woman's voice from the other side of the curtain.

"Missy, you calling fer me?" the man asks as he returns to the room.

"Who are you?" she asks.

11

He sets the water down and takes her hand, a strange wetness welling in his eyes. "My name's Matt. I'm yer husband."

He holds the cup to her lips and, when she seems to not quite know what to do next, he gently pours a little bit of water into her mouth. The cool liquid delights her tongue.

That is called a tongue, right?

After a moment of difficulty with her first time swallowing, she relaxes back on to her pillow. *Ohhhhhhhhh!* She feels the water slowly slipping down the back of her throat and then down into this body of hers like a living being itself. Cool meeting warmth, wet meeting dry, slipping down, down....

Could anything else in all the universes feel so heavenly? Ahhhhhhhhhhhh.

"Ohhhhhhhhhhh!"

"It's like you've never had a sip of water before."

Oh, you have no idea.

Matt lets out another strange noise.

That must be a laugh. But his eyes didn't laugh.

"Are you feeling good?" she asks. *That's not the right way to ask that question. Let's see, what was it?* "Are you okay?"

"Yes, Missy, I'm great, now that yer back."

His eyes don't match the words he's saying. Plus, what a strange accent he has.

"Why do you talk so funny?" she asks.

"I don't talk funny."

"Your name is Matt?"

"Yes. Do you remember me at all?"

She looks at him as if she's trying to remember his face. *You seem very kind but you are not who my project was supposed to be with.* "You're my husband, you said?"

"Yes, darlin', I am."

She thinks for a few seconds. "What's a husband?"

Matt's face falls.

After he leaves, she calls out, "Can I please come home?"

A nurse who'd been just down the hall sticks her head in the door. "We'll get you home just as soon as we can."

"Thank you," Missy says. The nurse leaves. Missy addresses the air over her bed with a much quieter voice. "Right now? Please?"

The old woman in the bed on the other side of the curtain responds, "Make that a double. I'd like to go now, too, please!"

Please? With starlight on top?

Ann Crawford

CHAPTER 2

Missy—as Missy is apparently who she resides in, although she wasn't supposed to—tugs on the tube attached to her hand and winces. "Ouch!"

"We might be able to get rid of that thing," the nurse says as she enters the room, "now that yer awake and can eat and drink."

She adjusts the bed so that Missy's sitting up, and she sticks a straw in her mouth. "Just suck, pull on the straw," the nurse instructs, clearly bewildered by how much she has to tell this woman.

Missy's eyes go wide as the liquid fills her mouth. *Ohhhhhhhh! That's nectar of the heavens!*

The nurse puts some lumpy-looking food item on a rounded eating implement and feeds her.

Ohhhhhhhh! Manna of creation!

"Most of my patients are nowhere near as appreciative of orange juice and oatmeal as you are!"

"Ohhhhhhhh, it's sooooooo good!" *Ohhhhhhhhhh!*

"Maybe everyone should have a coma so we can come back and be so grateful." The nurse feeds her another spoonful of oatmeal, to another swoon. "Okay, perhaps not. Perhaps we should just wake up every day and be grateful and skip the coma."

"I haven't heard the woman next to me," Missy says.

"She died last night."

"Oh! She got her wish."

"What wish?"

"She wanted to go home, 'now,' she said."

"Wow. Well, yes, she got her wish, then."

That makes one of us. As no one has yet to answer her beseeches to the ceiling, she adds, *Have you forgotten me down here? Just send me to the wrong place and then forget about me? Thanks!*

"Can you stand up? There you go! And how about taking a few steps with me? Hey, that's great!"

The physical therapist leads Missy away from her wheelchair, toward a walkway with two railings on either side. His skin is much darker than that of her family and most of the other hospital staff. She can't take her eyes off his arm.

"Missy," the older woman, who had identified herself to the young woman as her mother, says, "it's not polite to stare."

Missy touches his skin. "It's so beautiful. It hides all the blue lines and stuff underneath."

He laughs. "Yes, I suppose it does."

She looks at her hand. "I like it a lot better than mine."

Her mother rolls her eyes in a combination of embarrassment and relief that at least her daughter is breathing and moving and talking...even if the talking is nonsensical—and perhaps rude—at times.

"Missy," the physical therapist says, "I've never seen anyone go from flat on her back to up and walking so quickly after an accident like you had, plus the coma. Yer a miracle!"

"So are you," Missy responds.

He's clearly puzzled at her words, but smiles. "Perhaps I am."

So are all of you humans, really. You just seem to be the last beings in Creation to know it.

She considers this last thought of hers. *At least I'm warming up to the place. And them. Maybe.*

Missy smiles as she runs her finger along the flower's petals. So soft and delicate. A couple of the flowers are much larger than the others—yellow, with large, round centers and a thick...*Oh, I know that word...stem, right.* She runs her finger across the plush padding of the center and notices that it's not just the center of the flower; it has myriad little flowers all clustered together. *Amazing beings in their own right, these are.* She runs her finger along the soft, delicate petals of the pink and yellow flowers alongside the big yellow ones. *All of them.* She slowly explores the gentle folds, crevices, and interesting hiding places of a couple of the other flowers. *They must be roses.* She attempts her recall on the other flowers. *Perhaps those are daisies. Whatever they are, they're all beyond amazing.*

A nurse walks into her room.

"Liz," Missy says, reading her name tag.

"Yes," Liz answers, nowhere near as impressed as Missy is that she can read the letters.

Liz's darker skin, although not as dark as the PT's, as Missy's learned to call him, and features seem more exotic than most of the others. A thick, long, dark braid hangs down her back. Some of these words are coming to Missy; most others remain unreachable, like they're locked away in a section of her brain that she can't quite access yet.

"You can move around now, so you don't need this anymore." Liz starts to remove that very strange tube that had connected Missy's body to a bag hanging on the side of the bed.

"Ouch!"

"Sorry. It's not the most comfortable thing in the world. Can you go to the bathroom by yourself now? Do you need to?"

She guides Missy into the bathroom, seats her on the toilet, and leaves.

Missy's eyes widen, overcome with the relief of relieving herself. "Oh, wow! Oh, wow!"

"You alright in there?" Liz calls.

"Oh, yes!"

"Can I open the door?"

"Yes."

Liz pokes her head in, obviously flummoxed by the amount of joy Missy's experiencing in the bathroom. "Do you need to do anything more?"

"Maybe."

Liz closes the door again, and after an unusually unabashed big sigh and "Oh, wow!" that followed a few equally unabashed grunts and groans, she goes back in. She grabs some toilet paper and hands it to Missy, who is mystified by it. She shows her how to use it, flushes the toilet, and leads her from the room.

"That was amazing!" Missy raves.

"Uh, okay then." Liz's face flushes a bit. "Well, it's said that that's one of the best feelings we experience, along with the other expected ones."

"Like what?"

Liz's face flushes even more. "Sex. Eating. Fer some people the order is reversed, though," she chuckles.

After guiding her back to the bed, Liz fills a small tub with warm water. "I shouldn't have you try the shower yet," she says. "Yer still a little unstable."

She hands Missy a soft, squishy thing. When Missy just examines and then squeezes the article, clearly having no idea what to do with it, Liz holds her hand out. "Here, let me have the sponge back," she says and proceeds to wet Missy down with it.

"Wow—that's even more amazing!" Missy sighs as Liz makes gentle strokes on her face.

"Where in the world did you go in that coma of yers?" Liz asks. "Everything seems brand new to you."

Missy doesn't answer, lost in the rapture of the sponge cleaning her arms...her legs...and, oh, her back! And her front!

"Here's a ta'l." Liz starts to dry Missy's back and then hands her the towel to finish up.

Oh! This towel!

That night Matt sets a small, flat, rectangular object in her hand. When she's obviously perplexed by the item, he plugs in a long, thin black, bendable strand.

"Here, let's get these earbuds in." After gently placing the buds in her ears, he runs his thumb over and over the front of the object. "Let's see. What are yer favorite songs? Oh, here's one."

He turns on the device. Missy rips the earbuds out of her ears.

"Too loud?" Matt asks. "Sorry."

"No, not too loud. Whatever that is, it's awful!"

"What the hell? You love AC/DC."

"Uck!"

He shuffles through the song list some more. "Here's something a little mellower."

Missy places the earbuds back.

"I'm hungry," Matt says. "I'm gonna grab something in the cafeteria. You want anything?" When she shakes her head, he shakes his head, too. "You not interested in food. Now *that's* sure interesting."

After he leaves, she swipes through the song list, since Matt's version of "something a little mellower" isn't at all. She locates some music by Beethoven, a name she does remember from her training.

Strange I remember him but not a whole lot else—at least not enough.

She turns on the song. Wetness streams down her face as the exquisite sounds fill her ears.

Matt returns from the cafeteria. "Missy! You okay?"

She barely hears him, lost as she is in the sumptuous strains of the symphony.

"Ohhhhhh!"

Matt looks to see what song has her so enthralled. "What the hell? Since when are you into Beethoven? I didn't even know you had any classical music on here." He shuffles through her song list. "What the hell?" he repeats. "I didn't know you had a tenth of all this stuff. 'Amazing Grace' with Scottish bagpipes? And it's in Cherokee?"

"Oh, I'm just full of surprises."

That night, after figuring out how to use the device's store, she discovers John Lennon's "Imagine," Il Divo's version of "Amazing Grace," Carrie Underwood's "How Great Thou Art," and a host of other songs that had been included in her training. The tears stream and stream.

All those eons of training didn't prepare me for the beauty of the real thing. And not just in the music.

She's about to address the ceiling again, but sighs and turns back to her iPod instead.

Missy trudges down the hallway, holding the wall to steady herself. She looks out the window at the seemingly endless expanse of snow.

"Does it ever stop?" she asks a passing nurse, one she hasn't seen before.

"Does what ever stop?"

"The.....fields. Of snow."

The nurse's brows come together slightly. *Is that what they refer to as a frown?* "Well," she answers, "I suppose they do, sometime...at the Rocky Mountains, fer sure. But then you have even more snow."

Missy stares out the window.

"Yer new around here, aren't you?" the nurse asks.

"Oh, you could say that."

Liz walks by about an hour later to find Missy still staring out the window at the fields of white.

"We've had a lot of snow already this fall, much earlier than usual. Strange to have so much snow in November."

Liz leads Missy back to her room. "How about some TV? I don't think I've seen you watching much, if any."

She picks up the remote, turns on the television, and starts changing the channels. Missy's eyes go wide as the sights and sounds of big cities, men holding weapons, and children crying suddenly invade her quiet room.

Liz hands her the remote. "I'll let you find whatever you want to watch." She leaves the room.

Missy switches from channel to channel. "Ahhhhh," she says as a vague memory starts to surface in the far recesses of her brain. A glimpse of sitting with a group of beings watching humans on a similar machine back home flashes through her mind.

That night, alone in her room, Missy addresses the air again. "Is anybody there?" She waits a few seconds. "Can anyone hear me?"

"I can hear you," a nurse says as he rushes in. "Are you alright?"

"I guess so."

Perplexed and slightly perturbed, he leaves.

Missy speaks to the ceiling with a much softer voice. "Hello? I need help down here. This isn't exactly what was supposed to happen." She waits several seconds. "I don't think this is where I was supposed to be, and I don't seem to know as much as I should."

No response. She sighs and pulls the covers up to her chin.

This is going to be one long lifetime.

Ann Crawford

CHAPTER 3

The next day Matt drops off a couple more electronic devices. First he shows her how to use her cell phone, as he calls it, as a hotspot, as he calls that. He then reminds her how to use the laptop—or so he thinks, since he has no idea that she's never touched one before, at least not in this format in this dimension—and then leaves for the night.

Now that she's more fully on the planet, she doesn't need as much sleep as she did at first. She spends as much time as possible surfing (as she quickly learns it's called), Youtubing, Googling, everythinging to research these human be-things. She reads as many stories as she can, just to gain a better perspective.

Matt had brought up her Facebook account, and she went back to that over and over, trying to figure out what Missy'd had in common with the two-hundred and twelve people she was "friends" with. It seems like they all live in the same area, and that's about it. One, who she ascertains is her Uncle Charlie, makes her shoulders shoot up to her ears and gives her bumpy skin all over.

"Missy, you don't hold the mouse with yer left hand!" Matt says to her as he enters her room the next afternoon.

"Why not?"

"Yer right-handed!"

She tries using the mouse with her right hand. "Doesn't feel right." She moves the mouse and pad back to the left side.

After a nurse comes in to check her vitals that night, Matt follows her out. "Can someone go from right-handed to left after a coma and in the midst of amnesia?" Missy overhears him asking.

"Well, that sounds doubtful," the nurse answers him. "I've never heard of that, but I suppose anything is possible."

Missy's parents visit just about every night, as well. Linda clucks around the room like the mother hens Missy saw in some Kansas-farm videos. Frank never says a whole lot, but he seems sincerely elated to be there and to see his daughter come back to life. He wears a strange contraption around his face, which Missy determines is for oxygen, which comes from a tank he wheels behind him. Both of them have obviously enjoyed a great deal of food.

Matt's parents drop by a few times, but they never seem genuinely happy to be there—whether it's just in Missy's room or in life in general, she can't tell. She bets it's the latter.

Matt's father Bart is a red-faced man who seems to have swallowed a prickle, sat on a pincushion, or both.

"Just sit still and let me take that thorn out of your paw," Missy longs to say to him, for if he were an animal, that's what she'd suppose is wrong with him. She remembers reading about that fate in a fairy tale during one of her numerous marathon internet sessions. Reading fairy tales seems to give her the biggest understanding of and insight into these fascinating creatures, these human beings.

And Matt's mom Rita is even worse. Far more than a thorn in her paw, she seems to have an arrow in her heart. Rail thin like her husband, her narrow lips speak of a closed-off life. The pair doesn't talk much, and Missy counts the minutes until they leave. Thankfully they never stay very long.

Matt and Missy rummage through the bag of clothing items Matt brought from their house. He hands her some things that go on her legs—jeans, she remembers from one of her Google searches—and a warm, plush top—a sweater. The clothes hang on her.

"We'll have to get you some new duds," Matt says, "unless yer planning on gaining yer weight right back."

The sting lingers long after the words left his lips. He softens as he notices she seems to have crumpled, although it wasn't from what he said but from his tone. "Ready to go home?"

She nods. He walks her down the hallway and presses a button on the wall. A part of the wall opens up, revealing a little room. He guides her into it, presses another button, and after a few seconds the wall opens up again. He takes her hand as he guides her through a large, open room full of people and then out of the hospital.

"Oh!" Missy gasps as the warmth of the glowing ball in the sky hits her face. She shuts her eyes and tilts her head so her face receives the full impact of the star.

"I have an extra pair of sunglasses in the truck," Matt says. "My truck, that is. Yers is a piece of history now."

He leads her over to the pickup truck he'd just parked in the hospital's driveway. After helping her get settled in, including buckling her seatbelt, he asks, "How about we go to yer favorite eating spot?"

"That sounds good. You said you had some star-glasses for me?"

"Sunglasses." He hands them to her, somewhat taken aback by her disappointment over them.

Where I come from, starglasses are huge, sparkling, radiant things that help you see for lightyears. Oh, well.

25

Missy stares out the car window at the vast fields and fields of snow. *Earth looks green and blue from the Heavens, with just white spots at the poles. What is up with this? And what about those cities with buildings that touch the sky and those things that go over bodies of water, bringing people of different land masses together?*

She remembers being stunned by the videos of seemingly endless streams of people flowing into large cities. *I'd think that was on a whole other planet if I hadn't seen them on the television and computer.*

Matt drives to a tiny restaurant that's attached to a gas station, which also contains an auto-parts store. A vision of fine restaurants from some aspect of her training floats through Missy's mind. *So much for that.*

"This here's just a few towns over from ours," he explains to her as he leads her into the less-than-fine establishment, addressing her clear confusion. "But I'll be driving on a ways to yer mom and dad's place. It's just outside the next big town. Big for these parts, anyway."

"Where's the servant?" she asks as they sit down.

"Server! She's not our servant!"

Oh, right...oops.

Missy studies and studies and studies the menu, which has only about half a dozen dinner items listed. The server brings their drinks and then goes away and comes back—three times.

"Want me to order fer you?" Matt finally asks Missy. "I know what you loved." He gives the order to the server.

Missy studies the group of people at the next table. "What happened to their teeth?"

"Would you kindly lower yer voice, please?" Matt explains the side effects of doing meth to her.

"Why would they do something that'd hurt them so much?"

Matt shrugs.

"And why are those people over there soooooo big? Bigger than my parents?"

"Lower yer voice! Well, they eat too much and don't get enough exercise. That's not a good combination."

"Why aren't you as big as most of the other people?"

"Well, I keep myself super busy on the ranch and don't eat that much."

"Why doesn't everybody do something like that? It looks so uncomfortable not to."

Matt shrugs. "I don't know."

She looks over his body. "Well, your combination seems to be working for you."

He looks over her body. "One thing about a coma—it seems to help folks take the pounds off."

Missy ignores the slight dig. She's about to ask another question, but the server arrives with two plates heaped high with food. Missy does a doubletake at the mound of unidentifiable items smothered in brown liquid. She turns the plate around and around to see if there's a better angle on this mass of...whatever it is.

"Missy, you love chicken-fried steak. And mashed potatoes and gravy."

"Matt, this is more food than anyone should eat in two days!

"Well, yer not wrong about that," Matt utters around the food he's shoved in his mouth. "But eating a big meal every now and then is okay. And we can get a to-go box for whatever you don't eat."

Missy eyes some other patrons—not the too-skinny meth addicts, but the others—seated at nearby tables. "They obviously didn't get the every-now-and-then part of your statement."

"Shhhh!"

She takes a bite, though, and shuts her eyes in near-ecstasy.

"Now, *that's* the Missy I know," Matt says, but none too thrilled, apparently.

She can't talk, though, as she's completely enthralled by the sensations her taste buds are broadcasting out to the whole rest of her body. "Oh my galaxy," she whispers when she's finally swallowed.

"What's that?"

"Ohhhhhhhhhhhh!"

"Beats that hospital food, huh?"

But her mouth is full again already. "Mmmmmmmm hmmmmmmmmm."

After heading down the highway a bit, Matt pulls into the parking lot of a busy little café. The sign out front has a woman on it holding…something.

After ordering, paying, and waiting a bit, Matt hands her a large drink with a little mountain of fluffy white stuff on top, with stripes of brown dripping down the mountainsides.

"Here, got you extra whipped cream and lots of car'mul on top, just the way you like it."

Missy takes a lick of the whipped cream and her eyes go wide. "Oh!"

"Well, yer not supposed to lick it like an ice-cream cone. Sip it."

She does and then slaps her hand on the table.

"Missy! You okay?"

"Oh, my! How can you beings ever complain about anything?"

"How's that now?"

"Nothing." She takes another sip and moans again. Several customers seated nearby look over at her.

"Missy, sweetheart, can you calm yourself a bit?"

She takes a bite of the round treat on a stick he'd set down by her. The moans escalate.

"Geez," Matt says, trying to sink farther into his seat, "I feel like I'm straight out of *When Harry Met Sally*."

"Who's Harry? Who's Sally?"

"The main characters in one of yer favorite movies. You made me watch it at least half a dozen times."

She takes another sip and bite. The moans escalate even more. By this time everyone in the café is looking at her.

"Missy! Perhaps we should eat these in the car."

"Wherever you want!"

The customers in the café receive one more rendition of "Ohhhhhhhh!" as Matt leads her out the door and she takes another sip of her drink. She climbs into the truck as he walks around to the driver's side.

Okay, maybe it's not thaaaat bad here.

Ann Crawford

CHAPTER 4

Matt pulls the truck into the driveway of a tidy white house with green shutters and trim. The house would look lost and alone, surrounded by the vast fields of snow as it is, were it not for the lights beaming from every window. The next house down the road is barely in view.

Saddened by the lack of recognition on her face, he softly says, "This is the house you grew up in. It should all come back to you real soon. Hopefully, that is."

Linda waves from the walkway by the kitchen. "Get yourselves in here. Too cold to be lollygagging outside."

Once inside, Missy can't stop looking around the room—at the yellow gingham curtains, the yellow roses, the yellow tablecloth, even a big yellow vessel that says *Cookies* on it. The floors, counters, and surfaces look even cleaner than those in the hospital.

"It's so happy in here," she whispers to Matt when Linda goes into the next room for a minute.

"Yep. Yer mom likes to take care of her home some, that's fer sure."

Linda walks back into the kitchen and places on the table a small statue of a woman holding a ball, some ribbons with "#1" on them, and a picture of a much younger Missy hugging a horse. The words at the bottom of the statue read "Statewide Volleyball Champs" while the ribbons have a picture of a horse.

"Do you remember any of this?" Linda inquires.

Missy shakes her head. Matt and Linda look at each other and then back at her.

"I'll be fine," she says. "I'll remember it all again, I'm sure."

"Can I get you anything to eat?" Linda asks.

"I don't think I can eat anything until next week," Missy laughs.

"That's yer biggest change of all," Matt snips.

"Let's go into the living room and see if anything jogs yer memory," Linda says quickly.

In the cozy living room with light-brown furniture and matching carpet, dozens of framed photographs stare back at her. She spies one of a younger Matt and her, dressed up, with crowns.

"Were we a king and queen once?"

"We sure were. Of the senior prom."

Another photo nearby shows her in a stunning white dress holding a bunch of white flowers. Matt stands next to her in a black garment. She's smiling from ear to ear, but Matt isn't—not quite.

"Weren't you happy that day?" she asks him.

"Sure I was. I was marrying my high-school sweetheart." He sounds as convincing as his half-smile looks. "We was always Matt and Missy. Always meant to be together since the day we met, first day of high school." His words sound hollow—a phrase she remembers from her new friend Google—to her.

When she takes a closer look at the picture, however, she sees that Missy's eyes aren't smiling anywhere near as much as her mouth is. *Hmmmmmm.*

She looks at some more photos, including one of her father as a young soldier holding a large rifle in a jungle-like setting.

"My father was a warrior?"

"Yep. Viet Nam." When she doesn't reply, he adds, "That was a tough war our country fought about fifty years ago. It wasn't like other wars, though, like the one our grandfathers fought in. Yer mom says he wasn't ever quite the same after that. Same with my dad, according to my mom."

Linda opens one of the big window doors and an animal dashes in and over to Missy.

"Hello! Who are you?" She bends down, running her hands over the exceedingly friendly being.

Oh, so soft!

"That's Magic," Linda says. "He's known you fer almost ten years now. You've always been his favorite at any family gathering."

"What is he?"

"Half collie, half shepherd, all love," Linda answers.

That must mean he's a dog. Look at these eyes! He can see right into me, unlike anyone else in the room.

Magic backs up, staring at her, and then slinks away.

"Magic," Missy says, "it's okay." She follows him across the room, where he's ducked under an end table by the sofa. She kneels down and bends over, so they're practically forehead to forehead. "It's okay, my friend. Really. It is."

Magic hesitates, but then decides to believe her—especially since her petting puts him into sheer heaven.

She could practically hear him thinking *Well, she looks like Missy, so that's good enough for me.* But she knows that he knows she's someone else.

"Well, Missy Miss," Matt says. "I should get goin'. Gotta get some of the horses to Denver to trade. I'll be back in just a couple-three days. Like we told you, yer mom wanted you to come here fer a spell—maybe get some of yer old memories back. I hope it works. I'll be back in time fer Thanksgiving."

Linda walks down the hall and stands in a doorway. Missy joins her.

"Do you remember yer room, sweetheart?"

Missy just smiles. Several posters hang on the walls featuring people she doesn't know, but thankfully their names are on them: Shania Twain, Keith Urban, Garth Brooks, and Tim McGraw. And there's AC/DC, the band

Matt had mentioned back in the hospital. They don't seem to fit with the others, though.

The bed has nearly disappeared under a pink cover with a huge pink, fuzzy pillow taking up most of the space on the bed's surface. About two dozen stuffed animals sit at attention on the floor by the closet.

"We haven't changed it much since you left." When Missy doesn't respond, Linda sighs. "Perhaps you want to take a rest fer a bit."

"Okay."

Missy sits on the bed, and Linda shuts the door as she leaves. After poking through the closet, drawers, and bookcase and not discovering anything of much interest, Missy pulls out her laptop. She surfs for hours, gathering more information about these strange, if a little dull, creatures she's found herself surrounded by.

She awakens the next morning, fully clothed, on top of the covers, laptop still running beside her. As she climbs out of bed, she catches a whiff of herself.

"Oh! That's not pleasant!"

She pulls off her clothes from the day before and puts them in a basket on the closet floor. She catches a glimpse of herself in the full-length mirror and lets out a gasp of surprise. She looks down at her body and then back at her reflection. She turns to the right, then to the left, then even more to the right, and then even more to the left.

She gazes at her long limbs and then at the gentle curves and soft swells with interesting shapes, patterns and varying colors. She'd seen the human form during her training, but it's quite different seeing it in person, literally, as a person. She's nowhere near as big as most of the women she saw at the hospital or restaurant—or Linda—but not as thin as some others she's seen either.

This vehicle is amazingly beautiful!

The morning starlight—by now she knows it's called the sun here, but she prefers star, since that's what the sun is—lighting up the bedroom casts her in a golden glow. She turns and looks over her shoulder to see the back of her in the mirror. Her long, light-brown-colored hair—she could match the living-room furniture, too—falls down her back like a veil.

It's one thing to study human beings. It's a whole other thing altogether to be encased in this gorgeous piece of Creation.

She pulls on a robe that's hanging on the closet door—and then becomes lost for several moments in the sensual sensation of the soft, plush pile against her skin. "Ohhhhhhhhhh!" She slips into a pair of slippers and giggles as the softness caresses her feet.

She wanders down the hall to the bathroom, which is also very yellow with wallpaper, towels, fuzzy rug, and prints featuring that color. She examines the tub and the faucets, remembering coming across such objects in her Googling and Youtubing. She starts filling the tub, adjusting the temperature to something that feels good, and climbs in.

Holy Heaven!

Not only is the water pressing against her, head to toe, a sensory pleasure in itself, she also runs her hands over this luscious body thing of hers. Nothing in her eternal life had ever felt like this. "Ahhhhhhhhhhh!"

She explores the various parts of her body. Like the flowers by her hospital bed, she also has gentle folds and crevices and interesting hiding places. So soft and delicate, too—just like the flower petals.

A knock on the door breaks her sudden reverence for being a human be-thing. "Missy, you okay in there?" Linda calls.

"Ohhhhhhhh, yes!"

"You going to be out any time soon? You've been in there fer more'n an hour!"

"Yes!"

But then she disappears into the euphoria of toweling herself off. She rubs the towel over her eyes and gasps at the multitudes of shapes and colors that appear. *Oh my galaxy, it looks like my galaxy. It looks like home.* Then one single blue dot appears. *Oh, that looks like Earth when I first was coming here.*

She finishes toweling herself off, but then starts doing it all over again. *Who knew?*

Missy finally wanders into the kitchen.

"Missy, it's going on noon and yer still in yer bathrobe," Linda gently chides. "Want me to help you find something to wear?"

The two rummage through Missy's suitcase and find another pair of jeans and a sweater. Like the ones the day before, these hang on her, too.

"We should get you some new clothes, at least just a few fun things," Linda says. "Plus, I know it's a little early, but maybe we should buy our Christmas tree and decorate it. Maybe seeing the ornaments from when you were a little sassy thing will help spark some memories."

The mother and daughter (somewhat, sort of, at least here and now) drive to a big building. "Charlie's Feed Barn," the large sign declares. A few green trees lean against the outside of the building.

"Not a great assortment yet," Linda sighs. "I don't think I've ever bought a Christmas tree before Thanksgiving before."

The sales staff, decked out in their finest flannel and down vests, call out to her.

"Hey, Missy!"

"Missy, yer home!"

"Welcome back to the living!"

A woman nudges the man who said that last line.

"Where's Charlie?" Linda asks one of the workers.

"Ran an errand all the way in Wichita," comes the response.

"Who's Charlie?" Missy asks, once their new tree is strapped to the top of the car and they're heading down the road.

"My brother," Linda responds. "Yer uncle. You'll see him in just a few days on Thanksgiving." She sighs. "You don't remember that place, do you? No recollection at all?"

"No." But as on Facebook, the name *Charlie* causes a shiver to run through Missy's entire body.

"That's where you've worked fer the past twenty years."

"Oh."

Linda sighs. Missy takes her hand.

Coming to a halt at a big sign that says STOP, Linda puts her other hand on top of Missy's. "You haven't done that in twenty-five years." Linda wipes away a tear. "Oh, well, I guess we can concentrate on what we do have, as well as the new things yer bringin' back from that coma of yers."

Back at the house, Linda retrieves the boxes of ornaments from the basement. Missy follows her lead and they place ornaments on the tree.

"This was yer favorite, when you were a little thing." Linda holds out a sparking, elongated ornament with stripes of glitter on it. "It was my favorite from when I was a little thing, too." She sighs as Missy shows no sign of recognition.

"I'm sorry, Mom," Missy says.

Tears form in Linda's eyes. "You never called me 'Mom'—you only ever called me 'Momma.'"

"Momma," Missy says, throwing her arms around her.

Linda cautiously hugs her back.

Missy finds herself a bigger help in the kitchen than she expected to be.

I do seem to remember being trained in this. So where in the universe did all the other training go? Hopefully it's all on its way back. Soon.

Frank arrives home. He hugs his wife and daughter and sits down at the table. Missy and Linda set out on the table steaming plates of chicken, baked potatoes, a vegetable medley (from a bag in the freezer, Missy had noticed), and dinner rolls.

Linda and Frank join hands and Missy quickly takes the hands they hold out to her.

"Dear Lord," Frank starts, "we thank you fer this day and, most especially on this partic'lar day, fer bringin' our Missy back to us, raghtchere in our home."

The food is nowhere near as good as what she ate the day before, but eating itself is still a fun activity.

After dinner, Frank grabs a beer from the tall cooling machine and throws himself in a recliner in front of the TV.

"You like the Christmas tree, Frank?" Linda shouts over the noise from the television.

"Oh, yeah. Little early, isn't it?" He turns back to the TV.

Linda smiles at Missy's frown. "He's never been much of a talker."

"Maybe because the television is doing so much talking for him."

Linda's clearly distressed by her words but doesn't say anything.

Oops. Keep it simple. Just go with their lifestyle.

That night, Missy whispers to her bedroom. "Anyone there? I need help here. I wasn't trained for this one. Something's gone way wrong."

No answer emerges from either the Heavens or the closet.

The next morning Missy pores through the photo albums in the living room. She's gone all the way through the ones of her, from her infancy to last summer. She notices that the recent Missy wasn't nearly as slender as she is now, as Matt's frequent wisecracks attest to, but in her youth she'd been a bit of an athlete. Missy stares at the younger Missy posing with a group of girls with a volleyball and then another group with a basketball. She's just pulled out an album from Linda and Frank's courtship days when Linda walks into the living room.

"We were so happy," Linda says, looking over her shoulder. "Still are. But especially now that you've come back to us."

Missy browses through that album, and then she flips through the wedding album.

"Oh, to be young and beautiful again!" Linda laughs. "Didn't appreciate it when I had it, that's fer sure. Always wanted something else, something more, something better."

"Momma. You have it all now, still."

"Hungry?" Linda asks, completely ignoring what her daughter just said.

Linda makes three servings of pancakes for breakfast, throwing Missy into realms of bliss again. Frank isn't too far behind her, though.

"It's like you've never had pancakes before." Similar to the nurse in the hospital, Linda adds, "Maybe we all need to be in a coma to gain a new appreciation of everything. But," she says to her husband, "I'm not sure what yer excuse is."

"Just love yer cookin'. Always have. See you later." He leaves through the kitchen door.

"What does he do?" Missy remembers that phrase from many of her Google searches. *Just* be *more than* do, *Earthlings. You're human beings, not doings.*

Linda answers the question. "Farmer. This time of year he mostly meets with his buddies, though."

They spend most of the day in the living room with knitting needles and crochet hooks, as Linda called the odd-looking items. Missy rapidly picks up the intricate moves.

"I once heard," Linda says, "that doing crafts calms the mind. Gets you in a zone of peace, they said."

Missy is about to sigh, but stops herself.

Oh, wasn't I supposed to be doing a whole lot more than this? I mean, it's nice and all. Yes, very peaceful and quiet, too, compared to what I see on their television and internet. But....very quiet. Too quiet.

That night brings another prayer followed by spaghetti dinner (pasta with a scattering of meat and vegetables along with a pile of bread), and then Frank retires to the living room with a beer again.

"What was he like when you met him?"

"Well, I always knew him, growin' up in the same town and all. He was so much older, but everyone knows everyone, as you'll come to remember. He went off to the war with his buddies, like his father and his buddies did before him. But he was never the same after that."

"What happened?"

"Well, we weren't fighting a monster like Hitler that time around. It's kind of like they were fighting a monster they couldn't name. He saw some terrible action. Plus he accidentally killed a little girl one day, a toddler."

"Oh!"

"He didn't mean to, of course."

"Oh....poor Dad. And that poor family."

"He said the mother came out of her little home screamin' and tearin' her clothes. Like they say in the bible, she was rendin' her clothing—that's what she was doin'."

Missy looks over at Frank as he's absorbed in the television show.

"So I just let him be with his TV and his beer. At least it's just one beer."

Missy continues to watch Frank.

"We could join him," her mother says.

Missy follows her into the living room. Linda picks up her crafts basket and selects a needlepoint project to work on—a beautiful bouquet of roses.

Missy watches Linda do her needlepoint, then watches Frank watching the TV, then watches the TV a bit. Suddenly she feels as though she's being sucked into the television.

What the Heaven?

"I think I'll just go to bed."

"Good night, darlin'," Linda says.

"Good night, Little Miss," Frank says.

Alone in her room, Missy pulls out her laptop for another night of surfing and exploring. After a few minutes, though, she whispers, "Where are you beings? You have some explaining to do!"

A lot of explaining.

CHAPTER 5

Late the next morning, Matt returns from Denver. Missy notices he seems to be in a better mood than he's been in since she arrived.

"How's my Missy Miss doin'?"

"She's been sleepin' lots," Linda answers. *Well, not really. I just keep the bedroom door closed lots.* "And keepin' real quiet—not like the old Missy at all. Let's see, what else has she been doin'? Taking hour-long baths."

"Well, aren't we living the high life?" Matt teases.

Magic hangs his head and lumbers over to Missy.

"Magic must know she's leavin' today," Linda says. "He won't leave her side. Dang dog loves everybody, but this is something else altogether."

Missy winks at the dog...who winks back.

As the couple heads outside to the truck, Missy stops. "Oh, I forgot something."

She heads back into the house. Matt follows. A strange sound comes from the living room.

"What's that noise?"

"That's Andrea Bocelli. Yer momma heard him on *American Idol* a whole bunch of years ago and has listened to him ever since. She thinks no one knows."

Missy giggles. As she recovers from her surprise and grows used to the singing, she understands why Linda would enjoy listening to him. They move some of the kitchen chairs to make some noise to alert Linda they're back. Andrea is quickly silenced.

"I forgot my laptop," Missy says when Linda appears from the living room.

"You were never into computers before," Linda comments. "Of course, you were into a lot of other things before that yer not now."

"They'll come back. Maybe."

"Oh, that's just fine if some of 'em don't come back," Linda assures her.

Missy grabs her laptop, hugs Linda again, and leaves with Matt a couple steps behind her. She glances back and sees Matt giving Linda a big shrug of his shoulders.

"Or maybe you'll just have a brand-new Missy," she says to them, chuckling. "Would that be so bad?"

As Matt drives, she notices that some of the snow has melted, but the endless patches of brown fields depress her. Matt takes her to another restaurant where another mound of food is set before her.

"You trying to get me fat again?"

"You remember!"

She shakes her head. "You've made enough comments, plus I saw pictures at my mom and dad's house."

The smile that had started across Matt's face fades away.

After lunch, Matt pulls into the parking lot of another establishment.

"Dairy Queen? Will we actually meet a queen?"

"No, not really, hon. You have a special thing for their ice-cream cakes."

"My stomach can't hold another thing!"

"That's okay. We can take it home."

The sun is low in the sky over the plains as Matt pulls into the driveway of a very simple, somewhat weathered home. There are a few large buildings behind the house, plus animals off in the fields.

"Want to go see yer best friend?" Matt asks. "This food'll be okay out here in the truck for a bit."

Baffled, Missy doesn't respond. He takes her hand and leads her to the first of the large buildings.

A strange odor assaults her nose as he opens the large door, but comforting, soft sounds from the beautiful creatures bring a smile to her face. She knows from her late-night escapades with Google that these—and the animals in many pictures back at her mom and dad's house—are horses. But how much more magnificent they are in real life! Her smile stretches into a huge grin.

"You remember yer Diamond Girl?" Matt leads her to a beautiful brown mare with a long, white diamond shape in her fur between and over her eyes, going all the way up under where the front of her mane hangs down like bangs.

"Hey, Diamond Girl," she says. White shows around the horse's deep-brown eyes, and she pulls back a little as if she's confounded by this human who looks like Missy, but....

No, I'm not her. But I'm happy and honored to be great friends with you, just like she was.

Diamond Girl hesitates another moment, but then allows Missy—this Missy, anyway—to stroke her muzzle and run her hands over her mane.

Missy looks out over the fields toward the herd of cattle out in the snow.

"Aren't they cold?"

Matt shrugs. "They get used to it. If it gets really cold, they'll huddle up together and keep each other warm. Speaking of warm, let's go in the house. Well, after we get the stuff from the car."

Matt flips on the light switch and a plain kitchen greets her. She stands in the doorway gazing around the room, so different from Linda's: no cheerful colors, no flowers. It could use a paint job, too.

What's that word? Drab.

Matt takes the ice-cream cake from her hands and puts it in the freezer.

"I don't seem to take after my mom in homemaking."

"Nope. Sure don't."

"You never minded that?"

"Not so much." But the tone of his voice says he really did and still does.

She wanders into the living room. The couch and matching chair are gray. So is the carpet. There are no pictures in frames, no small trinkets lining the shelves. In fact, there are no shelves. This room makes the hospital room look like a party.

It's almost like these two people don't want to live here. Or it's temporary. Or...something.

She walks down the hallway to the bedroom, which has just a bed and a chest of drawers with nothing on top. She then heads farther down the hallway to the bathroom and spies another room, which seems to be just a holding spot for some random items.

"Why don't we have any children?"

"You couldn't."

Liquid springs to her eyes. *Oh! Wow, that stings.* "Why not? Doesn't every hu—I mean, well, why not?"

"Yer mom took you all over fer all kinds of tests. Never did figure it out. I got work to do with the horses." He leaves, rather abruptly.

She wanders through the house some more, trying to coax out a few of the secrets that live there. No such luck. They want to remain just what they are.

Hours pass and Matt still hasn't returned to the house. She's Googled, walked around the house some more, Googled some more, tried to whisper to the secrets some more, and finally climbed into bed.

Shortly after she turns off the light, Matt comes in. She hears him use the bathroom and brush his teeth.

She's starting to remember more and more of her training, and she thinks about the special ritual that two humans have together. It's the talk of the entire universe. Surely that has to happen sometime. But Matt just lies down in the bed with his back to her.

Oh, just feel that love. Not. Google is helping her develop an attitude.

Matt rolls onto his back and starts making those crazy noises. She studies the ceiling, growing brighter from the rising moon.

You can't just leave me here forever..........can you? You wouldn't..........would you?

Matt walks into the kitchen the next morning to find her in yet more ecstasy over a bite of ice-cream cake.

"Mmmmmmmmmmmmmmmm!"

"Cake fer breakfast?"

But she's way too absorbed in the sensations of her taste buds again to answer.

This is quite *the gig they have going here!*

She cuts off another piece of cake.

"Whoa, Nellie!"

"Who's Nellie?"

"Just means slow down. Maybe pace yourself. Maybe not make up fer three months of missing out on ice-cream cake on yer first day home."

A movement outside the window catches her eye—it's another humanoid. "Who's that?"

Matt looks out the window to where Missy has spied a man about their age heading toward the barn and stable. He's wearing that strange head garment that she's seen on other men, including on Frank.

"That's Tommy, my buddy who helps me with the horses and cattle. We have a bunch of reg'lar guys to help. He just comes over sometimes." He pauses for a few seconds, looking at her. "Do you remember at all how much you love riding horses?"

She shrugs and then starts to cut another piece of cake.

"Miss! Yer gonna give yerself a bellyache!"

"Fine." She puts the piece back and puts the cake back in the freezer.

"I'm going to take a shower." He leaves the room.

A few moments later she peeks down the hall toward the bathroom. Matt's left the door open but is mostly hidden by the steam on the shower door. His back is to her as he lathers shampoo on his hair.

Woah, Nellie! What in the universe?

The feelings flooding her body are incomparable, beyond anything she's ever felt before, anywhere.

Oh, you crazy human be-things! How can you possibly complain about anything, ever? Do you have any idea what you have going on here—on this planet, in these bodies of yours?

Relishing the scrumptious sensations in her physicality (still a brand-new dimension for her), she wanders down the hall. She stands outside the bathroom, watching intently, while Matt finishes up. Her eyes widen as he opens the shower door, reaches for a towel, and dries himself. He rubs some steam off the mirror and catches her watching him.

"Missy! You want to take a shower?"

"Sure."

He turns the water back on and holds the door open for her. Trying not to stare at his body, she slips out of her pj's—she remembers that term from one of her "friends" on the book of faces—and into the shower.

Ohhhhhhhh...my...Creator.

Utter euphoria fills her body as thousands upon thousands of tingles wash all over her. It's so much better than the tiny, slow shower she'd used a couple of times in the hospital. Matt leaves, shutting the door behind him.

She holds her hands under the spray, then lets the spray hit her face and her head. She pulls the shower-head from its holder and slowly sprays water up and down her arms and legs, down her back, across her front.

Ohhhhhhh...my...galaxy.

An hour later, Matt knocks on the door. "Missy, what in heaven's name you doin' in there?"

But Missy ignores him as she softly moves her face back and forth under the spray...for the hundredth time.

Matt opens the door. "You okay?"

"Oh, yes!"

"You done yet?"

"I could be, I guess."

"Fine. Here's a t'al." After she turns the water off, he wraps her in a towel.

Holy hallelujah.

Her knees nearly buckle at the sensation of his big hands running over the soft towel around her.

"Can we get goin'?" he asks.

"Ohhhhhhh, sure," she says, trying to not sound too disappointed. But even putting the soft clothing on her beautiful body are more moments of elation—well, except for that thing that clasps in the back.

As Matt drives into the middle of the small town, Missy notices something hanging off the very back of the pickup in front of them.

"Is that a sock?"

"Yep."

"What's in it?"

"Two tennis balls."

"Why in the universe—uh, the world—do they have a sock hanging off their...."

"Trailer hitch. That's what it's hanging off of."

"Off their trailer hitch?"

"Takes all kinds and everyone needs a hobby, I guess."

She recognizes the shape from seeing her husband just this morning and rolls her eyes.

Matt pulls the truck into the lot beside a very large, flat building. The parking lot is quite full, overflowing.

"Wasn't the most brilliant idea to go grocery shopping the day before Thanksgiving," Matt mutters.

Missy watches the stream of people walking in and out of the store.

"Ready fer yer next new adventure?"

"Sure."

"Let's get 'er done."

"Who's she?"

"Huh?"

"You said get 'er done. Who is the her you're referring to?"

"Hon, maybe don't say much until you get yer mem'ry back."

Missy is dazed as they walk the aisles of the super-market.

So many choices! Her extra-sensory awareness picks up something amiss, though. *Most of this food isn't real! No wonder they need to eat so much of it.*

When their cart is nearly full, Matt wheels it up to the front of the store, where a sweet young woman smiles at them. The machine in front of her sends out a strange series of beeps, almost like its own language... at least to Missy it's pretty close to a language.

Strange publications line the aisle on both sides of them. Missy can see that the headlines are falsehoods. *Why are they selling lies where they try to sell their nourishment?*

"Oh," Matt says, "forgot the milk. Could you just run back and get some? It's in that far corner back there. I'll stay here in case she finishes quickly."

Fifteen minutes later, Matt walks to the back of the store where Missy's still staring at the array of milk cartons.

"Missy, you alright?"

"Well, you said milk. There's two percent, one percent, organic, goat milk. There are big sizes, small sizes, in-between sizes. I don't know what kind of milk you want."

Matt reaches for the gallon of whole milk. "I'm sorry, Missy Girl. Shoulda just gotten it myself."

They slowly make their way back to the front of the store through the throngs of people. Matt tries to hide his irritation at having to wait again and on an even longer line this time.

"Let's get these put up," Matt says back in the house as they unload the bags of foodstuff on the kitchen counters.

"Put up?"

"In the fridge and cabinets."

Oh, put away.

"Where *did* you go in that coma of yers?" His patience seems to be wearing a little thin.

She turns to him. "Matt, honey, you happy I'm back?"

"Sure, Missy Girl. Of course I am."

Her expression conveys that his tone isn't entirely convincing.

"I am!" he repeats. "You happy to be home?"
She nods.
"You've had quite the journey."
That's sure the truth.

"Any day now!" she says to the ceiling that night while
Matt's out of the house, obviously avoiding her.
And this day would be good!

CHAPTER 6

The next day, Missy disappears into the shower again.

"Miss!" Matt calls into the bathroom from the hallway. "What the hell you doin'? It's one thing to be in the tub fer an hour; it's a whole other thing to be in the shower fer a whole hour! I'm amazed the hot water's been lasting that long. We gotta get goin' to yer folks' place for turkey dinner. Like now!"

Missy and Matt arrive back at the sweet white house where a number of cars sit in the driveway. Linda waves at them from the kitchen window.

After walking in the back door, Missy finds herself surrounded by a group of humans assembled in the kitchen. They're holding tight to clear vessels of various colored liquids and nibbling thin, crispy, crunchy things.

"Help yourself to potato chips and everything else," Linda says, seeming somewhat disheartened that she has to steer her daughter around the food spread on the kitchen table. "Want some pop?"

"Pop?"

Linda bites her trembling lip. "You've always liked Sprite the best. Let me get you some of that." She pours some clear liquid into a cup for her daughter.

A man about five years older approaches her. She smiles but returns to examining the food on the table.

"Missy Miss," he says, clearly crushed that she doesn't remember him.

"Yer brother Rod," Linda says.

Missy notices that one of those strange drops slips from her mother's eye down her cheek before she brushes it away. By now she knows they're called tears, but they're still odd to her.

Linda puts her arm around her son. "You remember him, don't you, Missy? Well, hopefully this will all come back to you."

"I'm so sorry I didn't make it back to see you in the hospital," Rod says to her, taking her hand. "But I called Mom every day to check on you."

"Montana's too far fer a quick trip, especially with a family and all," Frank says. "But at least we got him home fer Thanksgiving."

"Montana?" Missy hasn't studied geography as much as other things.

Rod puts his arm around a woman who's about his age. "You remember my wife Lori? And the kids? Here are yer favorite niece and nephew, Alison and Jim."

"Are you my favorites?" Missy asks them.

"Only because they're yer only niece and nephew," Frank says. "Gettin' to be a handful, almost teenagers and all."

"And look who's here over here," Linda smiles. "Yer cousin Leslie. You two were as thick as thieves."

"Thick as thieves?" Missy makes a note to study American idioms more in her late-night Google sessions, too.

"You two were so close, just like sisters."

A woman about her age approaches her and awkwardly gives her a hug. "You remember me, don't you, Missy?" At Missy's blank look, she continues, "We grew up together, nearly as close as sisters. I know all of your secrets, and you know all of mine."

"Your secrets are definitely secrets now," Missy says, and the group laughs—although not really.

An older man approaches her and puts his arms around her. She freezes.

"Missy, you remember yer Uncle Charlie, don't you?" Linda asks.

Every cell in her body turns to ice. She can barely look him in the eyes. Thankfully she gets a reprieve by another woman reaching out to hug her.

"And yer Aunt Jane."

"Missy, we're so happy yer back with us."

"And here's yer Aunt Flo, from Greensburg, where the tornado hit a bunch of years back. You have any recollection of that? The whole town was leveled but no one was hurt."

"Nope," Flo says. "We had enough warning that it was coming that we could turn off the gas and electricity in the whole town, and everyone hunkered down in their basements. And you should see how we rebuilt it! You'll get to see it this summer, hopefully, when my youngest gets married."

Missy smiles, as she tries to recall *tornado* from her Google searches. She tries eating one of the thin, crispy, crunchy things and almost gags. It's close to what she imagines the sea would taste like, since she's heard it's full of salt.

Whatever did my brothers and sisters do before the advent of the computer and the internet? Well, they probably didn't get rerouted after their training, that's what.

Missy and Matt walk into her parents' dining room and Missy stops, stock still. The side table is laden, overflowing with a deluge of food—a huge (dead) bird with a small pitcher of brown sauce beside it; large serving bowls of soft white stuff, elongated green things, and what looks like chunks of bread; several smaller serving bowls with some kind of red sauce; butter on a dish, dinner rolls, and a braided loaf of bread. An assortment of cakes and pies sit on a nearby table. *Oh, right.* She remembers from the chicken-fried-steak meal that the brown sauce and soft white stuff are gravy and mashed potatoes.

"Are we expecting more people?" Missy asks.

"No, darling," Linda laughs. "We'll just have lots and lots of leftovers. We'll be eating this through the weekend."

Missy watches Frank and then Matt load food—and then more food—onto their plates. She's more than somewhat dazed.

Linda takes her plate. "Here, let me help you. Here's some turkey, here's some stuffing, and here's some mashed potatoes and green beans. Here's the gravy boat—you tell me what you think is enough." Linda pours until Missy holds up her hand. "That's all? Well, okay." She butters a dinner roll and plops it on the mountain on Missy's plate.

The crowd can't all fit around the dining table, so some sit in the living room, balancing their up-to-the-stratosphere-high plates of food on their laps. Missy tries to focus on just her plate, eating around the edges and trying to get as far inward as possible.

The football game—*Is that a gladiator event? No, wrong millennium*—on the television makes it hard to hear the conversations around her, which seem a little stilted. The family members cast glances at her, and she just tries to smile back at them as best she can.

"Going back fer seconds," Matt says. "Want anything?"

Seconds? She shakes her head as her mouth is stuffed with stuffing.

Missy can only eat about a third of what's on her plate, and she starts to bring it to the kitchen.

"The doctor says she's never seen a case of amnesia like this," Missy overhears Linda telling Rod in the hallway between the kitchen and the dining room.

Missy lingers in the dining room, not wanting to eavesdrop but not wanting to avoid it either.

Uncle Charlie approaches her. "Sure glad to have you back with us, Missy," he says.

"Get away from me," she hisses.

Frank, passing by the dining room doorway, stops and approaches her. "Missy, everything okay in here?"

Missy considers hissing at Charlie some more, but thinks better of it. "Everything's fine, Dad."

Oh, it's so easy to lie here. No one can really tell. They've turned off that switch for discernment.

Frank leaves the room. As Charlie is about to follow him out, Missy says, "Just keep your distance."

Linda enters the room. "Are you done already?" She takes Missy's plate. "Ready fer some pumpkin pie?"

"Oh, I can't eat anything else right now."

"Alright. I'll take this into the kitchen. You go on back in there," she says, gesturing toward the living room. "Folks want to see you, all comin' back from the great beyond and all." Linda hurries toward the kitchen and Missy heads back to the living room.

"Missy," Leslie calls to her, patting the empty space on the sofa next to her.

Missy sits down. "Are you my BFF?"

Leslie laughs. "You could say that." She puts her arms around Missy's shoulders. "I live in Washington, D.C. now, and I never come back for Thanksgiving, but I had to come see you. I called Mom and Dad every day, and they called your mom and dad every day for updates all through your recovery. I actually burst into tears when they told me you woke up."

"You live in Washington, D.C.?" Missy isn't certain, but the name of that place seems familiar. *Wait a light year…wasn't that where I was supposed to go? What was I supposed to do there?*

"Yes, for almost twenty years now. I went to school there and stayed."

"Can I come visit you?"

"Wow," Linda says as she sits in a nearby recliner. "That's the most interest you've shown in anything since you woke up."

"Of course you can come visit," Leslie says. "You've never wanted to before."

"When can I come?"

"Missy!" Linda laughs. "We have to get you all better before you go flying off anywhere."

Missy smiles, but starts plotting. Plotting for what, exactly, she has no idea, but she starts anyway.

Once those crazy noises are emanating from Matt's mouth, Missy walks out to the stable.

"Hello? Hello? Someone has to be there. You can't just dump me down here, trained for something else entirely. Plus I think a whole lot of wires got crossed. Help me out here!"

Nothing. No answer, at least not from anyone other than the horses.

As she's drifting off to sleep a little while later, though, she feels herself rise up out of Missy's body. A being stands before her.

"What in the universe? What's happening? Where's my team from home? Who are you? And whoever you are, where in creation have you been?"

"I'm Bashiran and I'm your team down here."

"Not a very big team."

"And, yes, I do have some things to explain to you," he answers. "Your wires did get a little crossed."

"Why did you take so long?"

"Sorry. Time seems to take much longer on this planet sometimes. It really was just a short time—at least on our home planet—that we were trying to sort through your case."

"Do I have to stay here? I thought I had a much bigger job!"

"Well, I'm not certain. Don't you want to stay here?"

"Well, these people are tolerable, I suppose. More than tolerable, actually. They're kind of cute. But wasn't I supposed to—"

"Yes," Bashiran says. "You had a much bigger job. But maybe not, considering how much work there is to do here. And there. Everywhere, really."

"Can't I go to the other place?"

"Well, you've already started here. And there was a problem with your vehicle in the other place. I'll explain it all."

If anyone could've overheard their conversation, he or she would've heard a great, big "Whaaaaaaaaaaat?"

Ann Crawford

CHAPTER 7

"Tell me that again?"

Matt repeats the story of the virgin birth, the three wise men, and the little baby. They'd passed a few nativity scenes set up in front yards and Missy asked about them.

"You follow all that?"

"Not so much. Keeps people out of trouble, I suppose. Has gotten some others into tons of trouble, though, I also suppose."

Missy stares out the window as they drive to her parents' for Sunday dinner.

"I would've taken you to church this morning, but I thought it might've been too much, what with everyone wanting to talk to you and all. Thanksgiving seemed to be too much fer you."

"Thanks," she says. The story of Jesus still has her mystified, but she senses enough not to ask anyone about it.

When Matt starts snoring (she knows that word by now) that night, she crawls out of bed. She sets up the laptop on the kitchen table.

She Googles about Jesus and then creation stories from a number of different cultures—from the Dreamtime of the Australian Aboriginals, to the Greek and Roman gods and goddesses, to the Old Testament and the Twelve Commandments in the Jewish faith, to Mohammed's ascent to Heaven from Mecca in the Muslim religion. She also read about Shiva and Parvati with their son who was beheaded, so they put on the head of the nearest animal they could find, and thus the elephant-god Ganesh came into existence.

They all sound interesting. As good as any reason I'd come up with, I suppose. That's the good thing about Earth—you can make it up as you go along.

"I'm surprised this isn't part of yer muscle memory," Matt says as he reminds her how to saddle up her horse—introduces this Missy to it, really. Once she's settled on Diamond Girl's back, he leads the horse out to the riding ring.

"She might remind you how to ride, actually. You two were practically a centaur. You probably don't need me at all."

Missy remembers the term centaur from her studies the night before.

The morning sun is warmer than it's been since she's been out of the hospital experiencing morning sunshine. She looks over the barren fields, now with no snow. A few laborers are working in the other buildings and with the cows. "Why do we have this horse and cattle ranch in the middle of all this farmland?" she asks.

"Well, we inherited this land from my grandpa," Matt says. "This particular plot of land's too rough to farm—can't get a tractor and a combine over all those crevasses and such. So he raised cattle. A bunch of the aunts and uncles and then cousins who had horses brought 'em over here as they were movin' away. No one ever came back fer 'em."

"Lucky us," Missy says.

"Someday you'll remember all this, right? So I don't have to keep explainin' yer life to you?" Missy looks down. Matt sighs. "I'm sorry. Yer doin' yer best."

Got that right!

He guides Missy and Diamond Girl around the ring.

"Looks like she's gonna get you retrained. See, you don't need me after all. I gotta go downtown."

After he leaves in his usual abrupt fashion, Missy rides Diamond Girl for a bit—fast, slow, in between. Her Google researching told her the different gaits are walking, trotting, cantering, and galloping.

"You sure make life down here more fun," Missy whispers to the horse, running her hands through her beautiful mane. "Oh, it's not as bad as we all made it out to be, I guess. We shouldn't have been ones to judge. It's tough even just moving around in a body. Let alone all the other things these beings have to go through."

Diamond Girl nickers in agreement.

"You know what I'm talking about."

She gets the sense that someone's watching her. She looks back toward the stable, expecting to see Matt who might've returned for an item he forgot.

But it's Tommy. Her heart flutters slightly. *What was that?*

Tommy leans on the fence. "Mornin'."

"It is."

He chuckles. "That's shorthand fer 'Good mornin'.'"

She smiles. "Mornin'."

"You and yer coma are the talk of the town. You rememberin' much yet?"

"Not the particulars, really. Google helps with the generalities."

He nods, chewing on a piece of straw. He's about the same height as Matt, but where Matt is fair with light hair and somewhat thin, Tommy is swarthier with shaggy dark hair and is not thin, but isn't fat either.

She tries to recall some words from her Google searches. *What do they call that here? Stocky? No. Built? Yes, that's it.*

He also still has that strange headgear on, although by this time she's learned it's called a cowboy hat.

Again she wonders what the starbeings did on Earth during all those centuries before the computer age. *Well, they usually weren't left on their own like I was.* She grimaces at the sky.

"You sure seem to remember how to ride." When Tommy smiles, he gets deep indentations in his cheeks that cause her heart to flutter again.

She pats Diamond Girl's head. "She's certainly helping me out with the remembering." The woman and horse circle the ring a few more times. "What do you do when you're not here hanging out with horses?" she calls out to Tommy.

"Farmin'. Third generation here."

She stops Diamond Girl and looks out across the pastures.

"Wanna go fer a longer ride?" he asks. "I'll get Mystery."

Tommy heads back to the stable and quickly returns, leading the brown stallion. He opens the gate, hops on Mystery, and starts galloping across the fields. Diamond Girl follows him, without any coaxing from Missy.

Good thing this human body seems to know what to do here, because I sure as infinity have no idea.

Out on the far edge of the rocky fields, she notices a man sitting on the fence.

"Who's that?" she asks Tommy.

"Andy. Lives nearby." He's about to say something more, but instead he clicks to Mystery. The horse takes off at a full gallop again.

Diamond Girl does the same. With the wind rushing through her hair and the horse seeming to soar over the fields, Missy feels more alive than she's felt since arriving here.

A couple of hours later—maybe even a couple-three as Missy's learned they say around here—they return to the stable. Tommy climbs off of Mystery and holds out a hand to help Missy off of Diamond Girl. A bolt shoots through her entire body as she takes his hand.

This human body thing seems to have a mind of its own, that's for sure.

"Here," he says, starting to undo Diamond Girl's saddle. "Here, let's get this put up."

"Put up?" But then she remembers. *Oh, right, put away.*

"Where'd you go in that coma of yers?"

Matt pulls the pickup into a driveway of a rundown, ramshackle home. An equally ramshackle barn sits about a hundred yards from the house.

"Your parents live *here*?"

"Yep. Try to contain yer excitement. Gets worse. Way worse."

Way worse starts as soon as they climb out of the truck, and the smell of animal excrement reaches her nose.

"That's from the pigs. We'd always complain, 'Dad, it stinks around here!' And he'd always say, 'Smells like money to me.'" When Missy's expression shows him she doesn't understand, he adds, "Pigs are big money."

And as bad as that is, the inside is even worse—definitely "way worse." Just about every square inch of the house has something filling it, and even if no object fills the space, dust does. And while the outside smells like the pigs, the inside smells like...well, she's not sure what it smells like. Nasty, whatever it is.

Sitting in the middle of the mess makes Missy want to run screaming from the house. She's afraid to ask to use the bathroom, but the need finally grows too urgent.

After Rita directs her, Missy slinks down the hall, trying not to touch anything. She passes two bedrooms, also filled to overflowing. Both beds are unmade and look recently used.

Missy'd lost her appetite as soon as they'd walked into the house. But she makes herself eat the hamburgers along with French fries and corn on the cob (both from bags from the freezer; the bags are still sitting on the counter forming little pools around them).

"Does someone live with your parents?" she asks Matt on the way home.

"Nope."

"There are two bedrooms and they both look like they're being used."

She looks at him until he finally sighs.

"They haven't slept in the same room in many years. One night Mom woke up because Dad was stranglin' her."

"What?"

"He wasn't awake. He was havin' a flashback from the war."

"A flashback? From what war?"

"Viet Nam. He woke up one night to someone trying to strangle him, so he killed him."

Tears sting Missy's eyes once again.

"You people have so much to handle," she mutters.

"How's that?"

"Nothing. I'm sorry that happened to him and then to her."

"Yep."

They drive the rest of the way home in silence... although she notices that he looks over at her several times with a quizzical look on his face.

That night as they enter the bedroom to turn in, Missy wants to jump out of her skin. The feelings rushing through her are pleasant, but unpleasant. Warm but urgent. Mysterious but uncomfortable. Primal but peculiar.

She's completely addled, her thoughts in a jumble. Being with Tommy seemed to have awakened...oh, she wasn't quite sure what he awakened.

But Matt is your husband. Yeah, well, Matt seems as interested in me as he does the horses—kind of interested but from a caretaking perspective. And also from a distance.

"Matt, aren't we going to...well, you know...."

He seems like he's about to sigh but stops himself. "Whenever you want, Missy Miss. I'm just waitin' on you."

She quickly pulls her clothes off and hops into the bed. "You don't have to wait any more."

His mouth smiles, but his eyes don't. At all.

Hmmmm, shouldn't the male human be a little more excited at that prospect than this one's being?

Matt slides his pants off, then his T-shirt and underwear. Missy stares at his body, from the expanse of his shoulders to his knees, as the rest of his legs are blocked by the bed. Her gaze lingers at those interesting items at the bottom of his trunk.

Matt flinches a bit. "Yer acting like you've never seen me and my junk before." His chuckle does little to hide his discomfort.

"Junk?"

"Those things yer staring at."

"Why in the world would you call that junk? And, well, it's kind of like I'm seeing you—and them—for the very first time, you could say," Missy agrees. "At least in my new life here."

"Well, yer staring a little hard, Missy Girl."

"Well, let me, Matt. That's quite the body you have."

But he slides between the covers and then climbs on top of her.

"Uh, aren't we supposed to do some stuff beforehand?"

"Like what?"

"Oh, kissing, touching."

He kisses her hurriedly and grabs her breasts, none too gently.

"Ouch!" She sits up, holding the sheet tightly around her. "What in creation are you doing?"

He sits up, as well. "We can try this another time if you want," he murmers.

"That might be good."

He rolls onto his side, facing away from her.

The feelings flooding her body shift into a kind of pain, which confuses her even more. Tears of frustration slip down her face.

Once Matt falls asleep, she wanders into the living room.

"Bashiran," she whispers loudly, "could you please come back? Bashiran? I really need you. I really, really need you. Can I trade this project in for another? Please? This one's really strange."

Remembering that the last time she saw him was when she was drifting off to sleep, she drapes a gray blanket over her, curls up on the gray couch, and shuts her eyes.

"Please come back," she whispers through her tears. *Please.*

CHAPTER 8

"Hey, Miss, it's Les," Missy hears on her voicemail. "I never come back from D.C. this often," Leslie continues, "but we have some family business to take care of. Dad's not doing too well in the health department."

Missy presses redial.

"So we were as thick as thieves," Missy giggles later that night when she and Leslie settle in at the café with the woman on the sign.

"You remember!" Leslie smiles.

Missy shakes her head. "No, I remember my mom saying that at Thanksgiving. I remember everything since waking up. Just not much from before that."

Leslie stares into her coffee while Missy stares at the sign outside. She'd Googled the logo, trying to figure out what in the world the woman is—a mermaid? No, she's a siren; mermaids don't have a double tail.

"I'm sorry your father isn't doing well," she says to Leslie.

"His health has been on and off for years."

That's because he's creepy. Missy feels bad for having that thought. She knows Earthlings don't get sick because they're creepy—not at all.

But it doesn't help.

"Tell me about what you do," Missy says.

"Miss," Leslie sighs, "you were never all that into politics. You've been peppering me with questions for almost two hours now. No, I don't know the President. Or his family. What happened in that coma of yours?"

"What about Roberta Doyle?"

"The family friend? I know her a little. Why?"

Missy shrugs. "Just wondering. I've heard interesting things about her."

"Miss, I gotta go to Denver again." Matt drops a couple of bags from Home Depot on the counter.

"Take me with you."

"How's that now?"

"Take me with you."

Missy could see about a dozen thoughts cross over Matt's face—mostly distress followed by his mind trying to see how he could politely get out of that suggestion.

"Plus we can drop Leslie off at the airport."

"Miss, Denver is in the exact opposite direction of Wichita."

"Well, whatever. Just take me with you."

"Matt," Aunt Jane practically sings when she calls that night, "I hear you can take Leslie to the airport. I'd really appreciate that. I have to tend to the mister."

"Missy!" Matt groans when he clicks off the phone.

"Missy!" Matt repeats in the truck on the way to Wichita. "When did you get so interested in politics? I think Leslie's had enough of yer questions. Plus, she needs a break from politicking when she's not in Washington."

"It's okay," Leslie says in a manner that clearly conveys it's not at all okay.

Missy senses Matt and Leslie exchanging glances over her head.

They drop Leslie off, just as the sun sets, and head north to the interstate.

"Droppin' her off doubles our drivin' time," Matt grumbles. "Oh, well. Family favors come first."

"What about wife favors?" Missy asks.

"I think I've been givin' you one long favor ever since you woke up."

Missy slumps in her seat.

"I'm sorry," he mutters.

Nowhere near as sorry as I am. She rubs her hands, which hurt from cracks and roughness on her skin.

"We'll get you some hand lotion when we stop at the store," Matt says, obviously trying to make up for his rude remark.

I could handle a lot worse if there seemed to be more of a point to all this.

The interstate seems to be one long, straight line. Out in the blackness are about two dozen red lights, scattered across the horizon. They all go black for a few seconds, then turn back on. Missy's mesmerized by the sight. Red lights. Black night. Red lights. Black night.

"Some kind of intergalactic communication going on?"

"Uhhhhh, not exactly."

"What are those lights?"

"Lights on windmills. So no planes fly into them."

Missy watches the lights blink on and off. There's no moon and they're between rest stops with no other traffic on the road. Missy glances up at the sky.

"Stop! Stop the car!"

"What in hell's name—"

"Just stop!"

Matt steers the car over to the side of the road. Missy jumps out of the car and stares up at the sky. Back at the house, she's usually in for the night by sunset. Tears stream down her face. No longer the odd things they once seemed to be, the tears actually feel wonderful.

"Damn, girl. I thought you were in pain or something."

"Or something is right."

The wind nearly knocks her over—but it leaves the sky completely clear of any dust. The stars sparkle in the firmament.

I can almost see home. I want to go home.

Matt looks at his watch. Again. "Missy, we've been here almost an hour. I'm freezin'. You about done starin'?"

A light streaks across the sky before fading to black. Missy looks at over at her husband. *Or whatever he is.* She's starting to wonder about him.

"Shootin' star," he comments.

"Stars don't shoot," she replies.

He sighs. "It's really space debris—a meteor or somethin'—just falling to Earth and gettin' burned up in the atmosphere. Not really a star at all."

"I'm sorry you have to explain everything to me."

"S'aright."

"I'm sorry you had to take me on this trip."

"S'aright."

But it's not, at least not for him.

A few miles up the highway, they pull into a motel for the night. They set out early the next morning.

With the Rocky Mountains in full view ahead of them, Missy notices the clouds. "Look at all the spaceships!" She quickly covers her mouth.

"Missy, yer really scarin' me. Where'd you go in that coma of yers? Those aren't spaceships, they're clouds—special clouds: lenticular. They form that way because of the high winds from the mountains."

Missy nods but doesn't say anything. She studies the clouds carefully, as if looking for something...perhaps a friend or two.

Matt checks into a motel just off the interstate right outside of Denver, and they settle into a room. Missy examines the shampoo, conditioner, and soap on the sink.

"Someone left their bathroom items."

"Those're fer you."

"Nice of them to leave these things for us."

A couple hours after they go to sleep, Missy awakens. Noticing the empty bed beside her, she looks around for Matt. The bathroom is dark and empty. She opens the front door to find the truck gone from the parking space in front of the room.

Sighing, she paces a bit, then tries to go back to sleep. No such luck—so she returns to pacing. Then she tries sleeping again.

Finally she picks up the remote and studies it. She presses a few buttons, and after several clicks the television turns on.

Mesmerized, almost as intently as she was back at the hospital, she watches infomercials and ads and the headline news on CNN. Advertisements for food are interspersed with strange-sounding drugs in between reports of homicides and the odd natural disaster here and there.

She narrows her eyes as she studies the food and drugs. *Crazy system they have going here. Make people sick with those awful foods and then make them pay for drugs to try to get better, but they don't. They just get hooked on the drugs. And the food.*

She changes the channel to a pay-per-view of a certain category. She clicks "Pay" and her eyes grow very wide and her jaw drops as quite the steamy scene—with six participants—unfolds before her. Even more mesmerized, she tilts her head one way, then the other, and even forward and back as she tries to figure out what exactly she's seeing.

The camera focuses on one male-and-female couple who go off to the side to go at it. Missy's mouth remains open as the woman gasps and moans.

An hour later, Missy is still tilting her head back and forth, but with less surprise and bewilderment as before.

Something beeps and the door opens. Missy quickly changes the channel back to twenty-four-hours news.

"Where were you?" Missy barks at a very surprised Matt.

"What're you doin' up?"

"Where were you?"

"What're you doin' up?"

"Couldn't sleep. Where were you?"

"Just—out. Couldn't sleep either."

She turns back to the news. "I'll take sleepy Kansas over some of this any time," she gripes.

The next morning, Matt exits the motel office, hops into the truck, and slams the door.

"Missy, were you watching porn?" he sputters.

She doesn't respond.

"Did you click to pay fer a channel to watch people having sex?"

"I might have." Matt opens his mouth to speak. "I didn't mean to!" she says. "I wasn't quite sure what I was doing."

He stares at her for a few seconds and then starts to pull out from the parking spot.

"Nice to get an idea of how it's supposed to be done," she mutters. Of course she'd studied human lovemaking back on her home planet as part of the going-to-Earth curriculum, but the whole thing takes on a completely different perception when inside a human body.

"What's that?"

"Nothing." Long pause. "They sure did seem to be enjoying themselves."

As they pass the motel office, Missy glances inside—and lets out a gasp.

Matt cringes. "What's wrong?"

The front-desk clerk gives her a huge grin—no, not because she knows what Missy was watching the night before...her eyes flash a beam of light, a signal.

"Stop!"

"What?" Matt shouts, obviously wanting to leave the premises as quickly as possible. The tires squeal as he pulls out of the driveway.

"Please stop!"

He acquiesces, but none too willingly, and pulls into a parking space on the street.

"What's going on?"

"I need to go back there."

"Did you forget something?"

"No. I need to talk to her."

Oh, don't say that! These humans don't need so much truth.

"Missy, you crazy or somethin'? What's with you? What in tarnation do you need to talk to her fer?"

Tires squealing again, he tears out of the parking spot and heads down the street. When he stops at the red light on the corner, Missy jumps out of the car and sprints down the sidewalk back to the motel.

A bell announces her entrance, and the front desk-clerk appears from the back room. When she sees it's Missy, she smiles and flashes again.

"Who are you?" Missy sputters. "Where do you come from? How long have you been here? Are there more of us?"

"Are there more of us? There are millions of us!"

"Where are we all, then? You're the first one I've seen."

"We're all over the place. I'm Shamaeya. Here I'm Tammi. And you are—?"

Matt's face, red with anger, appears in the window in the door.

"Ashera. Here I'm Missy."

"You've got a wild one on your hands," Shamaeya says, motioning to Matt. As he opens the door, she whispers, "Just come back later. No sense getting him more riled up. I'll be here."

Matt drives to a big ranch south of Denver...and leaves her in the truck as he talks to the horse owners. Missy doesn't really care, although she knows she should.

Another night, another motel. After Matt leaves for yet one more mystery outing when he thinks she's asleep, Missy pulls out her phone and downloads the Uber app. She'd just recently read about Uber, Lyft, and the whole gig economy, as well as apps and the little store in her phone, similar to the one in her iPod.

The Uber driver drops her at the previous motel. She tries the office door, but it's locked.

"Need help?" a young man asks.

"I'm looking for Sha—Tammi," Missy says.

"She's off work fer the night. But she's in room one-twenty-six."

Missy dashes down the hall, forgetting to thank him. She pounds on her new friend's door.

"There you are," Shamaeya says. "C'mon in. Did he take forever to fall asleep?"

They sit on the two chairs by a table. A man snores in the bed.

"Actually, he was waiting for me to fall asleep and then he went out," Missy says.

"That's strange."

"Forget about him—tell me about you!"

Shamaeya's vehicle is a beautiful woman of Native American heritage, who appears to be in her late forties. She reveals to Missy/Ashera that she's been on Earth for almost thirty years. Her human was a teenager dying in childbirth, so she got to raise a child, now thirty and with a family of her own. Her husband works for the electric company.

"It's been a pretty good life, as these lives go."

"Do any of them know who you really are?"

"Oh, no."

"Why here?"

"Here's as good a spot as any. I get to see a lot of people in a day. I get to hand out lots of light and ease the pain in many, many hearts. Your husband isn't one of the ones I could reach—he's one tough case. Closed off."

"That he is." Missy sighs. "I'm on a ranch in western Kansas, in the middle of farm country. I was all set up for another project, but I got diverted to there. I lost a lot of my training in my descent because of the rapid switch."

"Oh, that's rough."

"How do I get out of there?"

"Why do you want to? It doesn't really matter where you are. It's all the same work."

"Well, my work was supposed to be a little bigger than on a ranch in a little town. I was getting trained in politics back home. You wouldn't believe who I was supposed to be working with—the President! But the family friend I was going to take over decided to live."

Shamaeya's eyes widen. "Oh, wow. That's quite a switch, alright."

"Tell me about it."

"It's okay, though. You can do as much work with the people you're around. Someone else will go back east. Just have fun with where you're at."

"That's the problem—what fun? I mean, some things are fun, but overall...." She stops.

"Well, sometimes you have to find it. Just call or text me any time. I can help you get through your basic training here."

As Matt drives them to a town south of Denver, Missy stares out the window.

It doesn't really matter where I am? I have to find the fun? Hah!

CHAPTER 9

The next day Missy finds herself in a huge arena with scores of horses. Matt, who seems unusually happy, introduces her to about a dozen people, but there's something about Derek that seems a little unusual. In addition to being the only black man in this sea of white cowboys, he seems...well, Missy isn't quite sure what he seems.

"How do you know Derek?" she asks Matt on the way back to a motel right by the arena.

"Afghanistan. Served together."

"That's nice."

"Well, no...it wasn't nice at all."

"I mean it's nice that you've stayed in touch all these years."

Matt doesn't respond. Missy doesn't push it. And once again he slips out that night when he thinks she's asleep.

The next night, after spending the day at the horse swap and Missy meeting about a dozen more of his Denver horse friends, he slips out again.

Unable to sleep, Missy pulls out the computer and starts her research.

"Missy, what're you doing?" Matt asks as he enters the room several hours later, awakening her as she was dozing over the keyboard.

"Oh, just looking at stuff." She notices that once again his mood is far better than usual. "Have fun?"

"Yep."

"Where'd you go?"

"Just out."

"You sure don't seem to need a lot of sleep when you're here."

He ignores her question and glances at her computer screen. "You looking up a word in the dictionary?"

"Well, kind of. Lots of words."

"Yer reading the dictionary?"

"Is that bad?"

"Well, no. Just kinda strange. You've never been into words much before. But if reading the dictionary makes you happy, by all means have at it."

The next night the entire scene repeats itself. Matt arrives back at the hotel room with a smile on his face.

"Still reading the dictionary?" he asks when he discovers she's awake again.

"No, the encyclopedia."

"Wikipedia, you mean?"

"No. I read that already." When he looks at her funny, she adds, "Well, not all of it."

"You sure don't need much sleep anymore either. That's the biggest change in you from before the coma. Well, the second biggest change. You weren't quite into reading the dictionary and encyclopedia before. Well, the third biggest change. You don't eat as much anymore either."

"What was I into?"

Matt sighs. "Yer horse. Yer job. That's about it."

"Was I into you?"

"Not so much."

"I'm sorry."

"S'aright."

"We must festinate," Missy giggles the next morning as they're packing up.

"How's that now?"

"It means go quickly."

"You can just say that."

"Okay."

Matt pulls the truck into their driveway.

"Meanwhile, back at the ranch and home on the range...." She chuckles.

Matt looks over at her. "You sure are different, Missy. That coma seems to have done well by you. You woke up a new person. Way happier."

Got that right. "Denver makes you a new person, too. Way happier." Matt looks at her sharply. Too sharply for the innocence of the remark, she thinks. "If you like it there so much, why don't we move there?"

"Can't leave my parents." He sighs at her puzzled expression. "You don't remember why, huh?" When she shakes her head, he sighs again. "You notice that picture of me at my mom and dad's place? The one picture in the whole house?"

Missy nods as she vaguely recalls a picture of a handsome, younger version of Matt on the mantle.

"That wasn't me. That was my twin brother Jason."

Missy stares at him.

"He didn't come home from Afghanistan. Alive, anyway."

Missy takes his hand.

"And they also lost a baby so many years ago, a girl. Crib death."

Missy kisses his hand.

"I can't leave them, too. It's been killin' 'em that we haven't had kids. Can't leave 'em. Just can't."

That night Matt tells her a bit about his tour in Afghanistan. He saw the accident that killed his brother and several friends. A plane was taking off from the runway and the cargo items hadn't been secured properly. Not long after takeoff and not high up, the cargo slipped backward and the plane's center of gravity shifted. The plane lurched into a stall the pilot didn't have time and space enough to recover from, and then it crashed. The man who'd been responsible for securing the cargo committed suicide about a month after the accident.

Matt stares out the window, flashing through his memories for a few moments.

"You all can't seem to get through this life here without a whole lot of pain," Missy comments, unaware of what she's saying as she's lost in her thoughts. She's growing quite impressed with these beings.

Matt looks at her for a minute before he says anything and interrupts her reverie. "We all? You've had yer share, too."

"Oh, yes, of course I have," she quickly says to cover over her last statement. "Just wish I could remember some of it."

"Maybe that's a huge gift you got."

"But who would you be without all that pain of yours? Aren't you a better person from that? More compassionate? More understanding? Life doesn't come without pain."

"I guess." He's quiet for a bit. "Who the hell'd you meet in that coma of yours, Jesus?"

· *Oh, I met him long before this life.*

CHAPTER 10

A few days after their return home, as they're getting into bed, Matt turns off the light. Missy turns it back on.

"What the hell, Miss?"

"Can't we see each other? Can't we do what couples do?"

Matt grunts a sigh of impatience. He drops his clothes quickly, slides between the covers, and climbs on top of her again. This time he kisses her lips, kisses her breasts, and then progresses a little more.

"Can you get on yer knees?"

"What?"

"Missy, what the hell? You usually like it that way."

Missy complies and Matt aims—

"Ouch!"

"Can't you do what you usually do to get ready fer me?"

"Can't you help me out a little? And can't we do this facing each other?" She lies on her back again.

He strokes her. A bit. Then he climbs on top of her and—

"Ouch! Matt!"

He climbs off and strokes her, a little longer this time. After he climbs on top of her again, his thrust meets its target.

Missy gasps, but more in surprise than anything else. She stares at the ceiling as Matt makes some motions over and inside her. She clenches her teeth as the motions start to hurt.

He stops, shutting his eyes as he climaxes.

He rolls off the bed, puts on his clothes, and leaves the room. She hears the front door open and close, and then she hears the car start and pull away.

Tears slide down her face. *These tears hurt. Well, the tears don't hurt—actually, they feel kind of good—but my heart sure hurts.*

It's after ten the next night when Matt walks in the kitchen door and then into the living room. Missy is completely engrossed in *The Wizard of Oz.*

"Missy, you hate that movie. No one in Kansas can watch that movie after age ten anyway."

"Ever notice the wizard shows up all over the place?" she asks. "He's at the gate to Emerald City, he drives the carriage, he's at the door to the palace, he's at—"

"Miss, you'd only know that if you've seen the movie more than once...since yer memory loss, anyway."

"I've seen it three times. Today."

"You a sucker for torture?"

"Ever hear the line the Munchkins sing about Dorothy falling far from a star? And the name of the star is Kansas?" *Just reverse all that.*

Matt heads down the hall to the bedroom, shaking his head. "I'm going to bed."

Missy follows him down the hallway. "Can't we....?"

The scene repeats, after some complaints from Matt. "What happened to you in that coma of yers? This is more than you wanted in the last few years put together."

Afterward, as he puts his clothes back on, she sighs. "Isn't there supposed to be more than that?"

"What're you talkin' about?"

"Aren't you supposed to help me.....aren't I supposed to enjoy myself, too?"

"Have at it. You never wanted me to be a part of that."

He leaves. She experiments some with her hand on the burning ember on this body of hers, sort of learning what he meant...but not entirely.

A few days later, Missy plugs in the vacuum and receives a big shock. "Ouch!" But she actually enjoys the feeling through her body.

She tries vacuuming, after returning to a YouTube video about housework several times. She dusts the house, although there are very few surfaces to dust.

When Matt arrives home that night, she follows him down the hall again. The same scenario repeats again.

"Matt, I need something...else," she says as he climbs off of her and then off of the bed.

He quickly pulls on his clothes. "You usually want to be left to yer own devices—like, literally. You always said you preferred it that way."

Her face clearly registers absolutely no understanding of what he's talking about. Matt opens a drawer in the nightstand, pulls something out, and drops it on the bed. And leaves.

Missy picks the item up and examines it. She'd come across it before, in her explorations of the house, but since she had no comprehension of the product, she didn't pay any attention to it. She locates the on switch and is surprised to hear a loud buzz. She presses it against her arm, then her stomach, then that fiery, tingling part below. She's utterly amazed to discover how loud these human vocal chords of hers can get—even louder than the woman in the movie back in the motel outside of Denver.

And she finds herself in a much better mood after that. "*Definitely* quite the gig they have down here," she says to Diamond Girl the next morning.

Missy rides Diamond Girl to the far edges of the property. Something moving in the shadows of the trees catches her attention. A man sits on the fence, like he's been waiting for her.

"Hey, Miss."

"Hi." She pulls up on the reins. "Do I know you?"

"Yep. You sure do." He walks over to her and puts his hand on her leg.

She brushes his hand away. "I'm guessing I know you kinda well."

"Yep. Hopefully it'll come back to you soon. Been missin' you somethin' awful."

She notices that some of his teeth are missing, like the meth addicts she saw in the restaurant her first day out of the hospital. He also smells horrible. "What's your name?"

The man's eyes register extreme sadness. "Andy."

"Oh, Tommy pointed you out to me one day, I think." Diamond Girl starts back toward the barn as if on a mission, and Missy doesn't interfere with her sudden quest. "Bye, Andy," Missy calls over her shoulder.

"See you soon, I hope," he calls after her.

"Missy, what in the Sam Hill you buyin' from Amazon all day long? And where the hell did you take an Uber? Our credit-card bill is four-hundred dollars!"

"Oh, mostly books."

"Since when have you been so into books?"

"Matt, who's Andy?"

Matt almost spits out the water he'd started drinking. "He been comin' around here?"

"I saw him on the far edge of the property."

"Well, let's hope he stays way out there."

Missy's usual curiosity and contrariness keep quiet.

Matt finishes his water. "Can you check some books out of the library instead of buyin' 'em?"

"Library?" She's grateful he seems to have forgotten his question about the Uber rides.

"A place where you can check out books for free. I'll show you."

"I guess. But don't we have plenty of money from the accident?"

Missy had been injured and her car totaled by a hit-and-run driver, but the accident had been caught on video camera. The other person's insurance company is paying all the medical bills plus covering her post-hospital convalescence.

"Yeah, but still. When I gave you yer purse with the credit card, I didn't think you'd go hog wild with it. I'll drop you off at the library tomorrow."

Missy wanders through the library, looking at the shelves and shelves of books. She studies the history books, then ambles over to the philosophy section. Next comes the religion section, and then she moves on to the new-age section. She picks up a couple of books about aliens.

"As if!" Google has taught her a few choice expressions.

She wanders down the sidewalk and into the coffee shop. She orders one of those whipped-cream-covered, caramel-drizzled coffee drinks that Matt had bought for her on her first day out of the hospital. She starts to leave the café but spots Andy walking down the street. She stays inside until long after he passes.

That night she buys a few more books on Amazon to avoid having to go downtown.

I don't want to see that guy again. He's got a few dark shadows attached to him.

Ann Crawford

CHAPTER 11

The next time the bedroom scene repeats itself, a few days later, she's the one to roll away first. "I always thought it was supposed to mean more," she sighs.

Matt freezes in the midst of zipping his jeans, his face scrunched in confusion. When she notices he's stopped moving, she looks back at him. As he stares at her, the scrunchiness switches to shock.

She turns away from him, sheer dread crossing her face as she realizes her mistake.

"I didn't mean that—" she starts. She looks over her shoulder at him.

Shock has now switched to trepidation. "Yer not her," Matt whispers.

She sits up. "What are you talking about?"

He backs up. "Who are you?"

"You know who I am."

"No...no, I don't." His face goes white. "I don't have any idea who you are," he whispers. "I just know who yer not, and yer not her. It just hit me. I mean, you been sayin' and doin' weird things all along, but it really just finally hit me."

She starts to speak again, but his expression informs her that it's no use. She wants to continue denying it, but it's clear that no words could change his mind.

"It's not just this, here...this stuff in the bedroom," he says in a low voice. "It's—other stuff, too. The books, the constant Googling. But mostly here. Plus, you've said some really bizarre things, but that last one beats all." He stands against the wall like a cornered animal.

A long while passes before she says anything. "How did you know it all wasn't Missy's amnesia?"

"Missy never cared in here. Not one minute. We were together maybe once or twice a year. That's it."

"But so many things can change after a coma, after amnesia, after any accident or medical incident, really."

Tears spring to his eyes. "I knew you weren't her. I somehow knew it fer a while but didn't...I don't know. But I do know yer not Missy. Who are you?"

"I can't tell you."

"Can't or won't?"

"Can't."

He throws on the rest of his clothes and vanishes from the room. The front door slams.

I really hate it when he does that.

But she really doesn't blame him this time.

A couple of days later, the front door opens again. Missy's trying her hand at scrubbing the kitchen floor, but she's made a minor flood.

Matt grabs the mop from the utility rack in the closet and opens the back door, pushing the water out. Cold air blows into the room.

Once the kitchen-cleaning fiasco is tended to, they wander into the living room. The day matches the gray furniture, although Missy has picked up some beautiful cut flowers and a pair of small poinsettias at the nearest store...which was four miles round trip, but her first long walk did her well.

"Why can't you tell me?" Matt demands. "It's not like I don't know now."

"I'll tell you," she sighs. "Since you know anyway."

"Not sure I want to hear it now." His shaky laugh betrays his nervousness. "How is somethin' like this even possible?"

"It happens all over the place, all the time."

"Great. Those crazy people are right about their aliens."

"Call me a starbeing. It's a lot friendlier sounding than alien."

He thinks for a few minutes and she doesn't push him. "I knew, somehow," he finally says. "Actually, I knew right away."

"How?"

"Yer...more...here...than Missy ever seemed to be. It was like she had a foot out the door already."

"Hmmmmmm." Missy pauses. "You go to Denver?"

He looks at her. "How'd you know? Do you know things without being told?"

"Well, I'm kind of supposed to know a lot of things without being told, but I got really messed up during my descent."

"Lucky me. I'm teasin', I'm teasin'," he quickly says to her crestfallen face. "What's yer real name?"

"Asheratavidelpinom Vasieranigolminradtrun Shanlondamispheria Rosqualyanira...."

A full minute later, she finally finishes her name.

"I was gonna cut you off," Matt chuckles, "sayin' I got the gist and all, but I figure it's polite to hear folks state their full name."

"That was very polite of you. Especially since my name is eight hundred and ninety-two syllables."

"Can I just call you Missy?"

They laugh, but Matt stops abruptly. "Actually I can't call you Missy if yer not her." She nods. "But I can't call you anything else, either—at least not in public."

She shrugs and nods again. "There is a 'Mis' in there. Just pick up on that."

"There's a whole lot in there," he snickers. "I could pick up on any name I want, just about. I heard an Amy and a couple-three Annies in there."

"Beings on my home planet call me Ashera."

"I can't exactly start calling you Ashera. Folks'd sure look at us funny."

She giggles. They both turn and lean on the back of the couch, staring out at the dark clouds looming in the West.

"'nother snowstorm's brewin'."

"Why didn't your people choose a friendlier part of this planet?"

"Just wait until spring. You'll change yer tune. It's beautiful here most of the year." He pauses. "Where do you come from?"

"Far away. In the Andromeda Galaxy."

"Is it very different from here?"

"Very. We don't have physical bodies. There's no density. Every thought is broadcast, so there's no way to hide anything. That's just the beginning of the differences."

Matt's quiet as he digests that. "Where'd she go?" he finally asks. "What did you do with her?"

"I didn't do anything with her. She was leaving anyway."

"You mean she died?"

"Yes."

He rests his head on his arm, which is resting along the back of the couch.

"She's fine," she says, touching his shoulder. "Most humans who die are just fine."

"Most?"

"Some aren't. Depends what they want to put themselves through for what they put other people through while they were here."

Matt thinks about that for a minute. "You mean Hell?"

"Of their own making."

Matt picks at the fabric on the couch for a bit. "How would her body have been strong enough fer you to take it over but not enough fer her to stay in it?"

"You know, you're picking this up and accepting it a lot faster than most beings around here would, I think. You're asking great questions, too. The human body is an amazing creation. Some people are just done here.

But that doesn't necessarily mean the body has to be done."

"Why was she done?"

"I don't know. I was supposed to know everything about the person I was taking over." She quickly places her hand over her mouth, and her eyes go wide as she realizes her new mistake.

"What? Whatchou talkin' about?" He jumps up off the couch. "You wasn't even supposed to be Missy? So much fer me pickin' this up and acceptin' it so great—I can't take all this!"

The door slams again.

Braving the snowstorm, Missy heads out to the stable. The horses poke their heads over the stall walls, obviously hoping for some food. She takes down the food sack hanging by the door.

After giving them all a treat, she stands by Diamond Girl. She nuzzles her muzzle, pressing her cheek against the horse's face.

"Bashiran, you around?" she calls out. "Are you there? I am completely messing up this project! So much for being incognito."

No answer, although the barn cats rustling in the rafters raise her hopes for a few seconds. She turns back to her friend and throws her arms around her neck, letting Diamond Girl's glorious mane absorb her tears.

"Missy, whatchou doin'?" Tommy stands in the doorway of the stall, the sunrise streaming in through the window behind him. "Matt must be lookin' all over fer you."

"No, he had to go out last night."

That isn't exactly right. But it isn't exactly wrong, either. Wow, this human deception thing is so easy to fall into. Well, what's deceptive, anyway?

On Missy's home planet, as she started to tell Matt, nothing deceptive can be said because the other beings can read energy so well—there's no point. The true intent of words, even thoughts, can be read immediately. It can be quite inconvenient at times.

"Can I help you up?" Tommy says as Missy struggles getting to her feet.

"Sure."

A bolt of electricity charges through her as he takes her hand.

Oh, that's not good. I mean it's good; it's great; it's beyond magnificent. But that's so not good.

And it gets even worse as Tommy helps brush off the hay stuck to her jacket. Oh, how different it is when a touch isn't detached! Every cell in her body is fully charged, like when she got shocked by the vacuum cleaner's plug. But this was better. So much better.

Hello.

CHAPTER 12

A few mornings later, Missy waits until Tommy parks his pickup and disappears into the stable, and then she walks down the path. In addition to being lonely and tired of being alone in the house, she's crazy longing to see him again.

She even Googled him the previous night. She found his last name in a box of Matt's financial paperwork for the ranch. Good thing there aren't too many Tommy Zysk's in Kansas...or anywhere, really.

Woah, Nellie! Was that him—that studly roadie for some country band fifteen years ago? But even more than studying his tight T-shirt over that buff body, she studied his easy smile, his easy way of being...so much easier than most humans seem to be.

He has that easy smile flashing this morning. Plus it doesn't hurt that he looks even better now than he did back then. In between feeding the horses, he scratches their ears and runs his hand over their muzzles and manes.

"Hey, handsome," he says to Mystery. "That tastes good, huh?"

Tommy is an amalgam of so many clichés that Missy's discovered—in amongst discovering words like *cliché.* The rugged individualist. The Lone Ranger—not the TV character so much, but definitely some kind of mild-mannered superhero in disguise. *Oh, wait, that's Super-man.* The Marlboro Man, too, except he doesn't smoke.

He notices her standing in the doorway. "Mornin', Miss."

"It is."

They laugh. He has a piece of straw in his mouth. Missy breaks off a piece and sticks it in her mouth.

He chuckles again. "Looks good on you." He notices a book under her arm. "Watcha readin'?"

"*A Brief History* of Time by Stephen Hawking."

"That's a good one."

"You read this?"

"Yep."

"Tommy, you don't talk a whole lot."

"Nope."

"But you sure know a whole lot."

"Yep. I don't say much. Most folks think I'm simple. I just let 'em go ahead and think that. In fact, the rest of the country thinks those of us in these parts are plain and simple if not outright stupid. But we might surprise a few folks. We're right in the heart of America. No one's more centered than we are."

She smiles at him. "Hmmmmmm." *Actually, many beings in the Universe think that about this whole planet, but how wrong they are.*

"Where're you gonna read, anyway?"

"With Diamond Girl." She doesn't tell him that she far prefers reading in the stable in Diamond Girl's company to the starkness of her house.

She wanders over to the stable doors. "Oh, it's such a pretty day."

"Yer a pretty day." Tommy quickly stops himself. "I'm sorry. I shouldn't have said that." He starts to leave.

"Tommy, you got a woman in your life?"

"Yep."

"Oh."

"More'n one."

"Really?"

"There's my mom, my sister, my cousins, my—"

"Oh, you know what I mean."

"Nope."

"Why not?"

"Found one a long time ago. She died a few years back."

"Oh! I'm so sorry."

She follows him down the line of horses as he gives each one of them a treat. He starts to saddle up one of the mares.

"Tommy, can you and I ever...well...get together?"

"Woah, Missy! Whatchou talkin' 'bout?"

"Oh, you know...." She puts her hands on his shoulders.

Surprise drains the color from Tommy's face. "Missy, yer a married woman. I'm really sorry fer what I just said a minute ago. I shouldn't've said it. But what the hell did that coma do to you? You can't be messin' around."

"Messin' around?"

"You can't be with other men! Not with this man, anyway." The sharpness in his last sentence surprises her.

"Why not? Isn't love supposed to be shared?"

"Sure it is—with yer husband!"

She sighs and tosses the straw to the ground. "Love is meant to be shared more than that."

"It's also meant to go deep, which it can't do if it's spread around a whole lot. Go deep with one person—yer husband, like I said."

"You don't seem like the type to be all into rules and regulations."

"I'm not. I'm into agreements. Can't go messin' with agreements."

"Tommy—it's not like...." She stops.

"You can always change agreements. But until then, messin' with them just leads to one, big, well, mess."

"I didn't make an agreement with that man." She hides her gasp as she realizes she might've said too much.

"Yeah, ya did. Even if you didn't mean to. It's still there."

He finishes saddling up one of the horses, jumps on her, and heads out to the fields.

He calls back to her over his shoulder. "Lemme know when the agreement changes."

Later that night, Matt returns home and completely avoids her. After waiting impatiently for his snores to fill the house, Missy dashes to the stable. Once again she doesn't even want to wait until she's falling asleep.

"Bashiran! Bashiran! Are you here? Please come talk to me! Is anyone there?"

There's no answer, only the soft snorts of the horses.

She walks over to one of the horses and runs her hand over his mane. She runs her fingers over his muzzle and even rubs her cheek against the velvety soft area of his nose.

"Who would've thought Earth could be so absolutely crazy hard?" she asks the horse.

He whinnies a sympathetic response.

The next day, after a short trip to town, Matt pulls back into the driveway. He doesn't emerge from the car for a long while, though. Standing by the kitchen window, Missy watches him softly punch the steering wheel.

When he finally does come into the house, he doesn't say anything to her. He just heads to their room, then takes a shower, then heads to their room again.

She Googles until he finally enters the kitchen again.

"Want some coffee?"

"Sure."

A word. At least it was something.

Their steaming cups of coffee sitting on the very aptly named coffee table, the two sit backwards on the couch again, leaning along the back, staring out the window. The endless fields of snow have been even more freshened up by an early-morning snowfall.

"When you look at Earth from far away, it's mostly blue. With a lot of green." Missy sighs. "This isn't either."

"Well, you must not've been lookin' too close. Or you must've been lookin' at Florida or California or someplace near water with lots of lawns and palm trees, or African or South American jungles. And whatever it was, you weren't lookin' at winter. Why in creation would you choose to come to Kansas in the wintertime?"

Missy smiles at his use of *creation.*

"I thought starbeings would be smart," Matt continues. "I mean—yer smart, but you have to be told a lot of things. Don't you get some training before you get sent here?

"First of all, how often have you thought of starbeings? Second, as I told you, I somehow lost a lot of my training in my descent. That's not supposed to happen."

"Like I said before, lucky me." He quickly adds, "I'm still teasin'. But I'll tell ya, I've thought about starbeings a lot in my life. Can't have this big sky stretchin' from horizon to horizon, full of stars and planets and strange lights sometimes, without thinkin' about what might be out there...and the possibility of starbeings."

Missy nods as she considers this. "Then you're just as crazy as those crazy people you were talking about."

"Nah. I'm not as public with my crazy as they like to be."

She considers that, and then she continues her list. "Third, as you know, I was supposed to be someone else."

"Right. Can you tell me who you were supposed to be?"

"I was supposed to be one of the President's family's best friends, from New York City."

"And you thought *I* talked funny?"

"Not all New Yorkers have that accent. The friend doesn't. She was going to die, and I was fully trained to be her, not a Kansas farmwife."

"Ranchwife, since yer goin' there."

"Not that there's anything wrong with that," she quickly assures him.

"Damn good thing you ended up in Kansas with all these crazy questions of yours, and not knowin' how anything works around here. It's a lot easier to learn here than in a big city."

"After I was to take over the friend," Missy continues, "I was going to move to Washington, D.C. and kind of be, well, in the thick of things. An agent of change, you could say. Someone who could make a huge difference."

"What would you have done there?"

"Lots. And lots. And then more lots."

Matt considers this. "So what happened?"

"She lived."

Matt laughs dryly. "And Missy didn't."

"No."

"Well, like I said, if yer havin' a hard time in sleepy, peaceful Kansas, how would you have handled New York City? And Washington, D.C.?"

"But I was trained for all that. And then I lost it in the rapid switch during my descent."

"Descent. Sounds like you ended up in Hell."

Missy shoots him a look.

"Yeah, maybe you did end up in Hell."

Missy doesn't respond. Matt heads to the barn.

Later that afternoon, as they head out to do some Christmas shopping, Missy's mesmerized by the lights on the homes.

"It's really not Hell here," she smiles, "if you just focus on the lights."

Matt pulls into the drive-through of a fast-food place and orders for both of them. He then pulls into a parking space where they start eating their dinners.

"You know this food is hardly food, right?"

Matt sighs. "I wish you had gone to New York or D.C. It'd been easier if she'd just stayed in the coma and then died."

"Then you could've been the grieving widower and everyone'd leave you alone, huh?"

He casts his face down, making his answer obvious.

"Matt, you don't prefer women, do you?"

He looks over at her. "What in the world makes you say that?" But obviously by the expression on her face, he gauges that his jig is up, too. "How'd you know?"

"Just did. I'm not bad looking and you just look right through me like I mean nothing to you. Not when we're just having conversations, but definitely when it comes to the bedroom."

Matt throws the uneaten portion of his burger into the bag and stares out the window.

"Did Missy know?"

He doesn't answer.

"Really would've been better for you if Missy'd just gone ahead and died, huh?"

He looks over at her again and then bursts into quiet tears.

"Yes, you could've been the grieving widower," Missy repeats, "and folks would pretty much leave you alone. Then you could've gone on with your quiet life, like visiting Derek in Denver."

He looks over at her, surprise showing through his tears. "How did you know it was him?"

"You're always so happy after those trips. You have so much more patience with me when you get back from there. I knew it was someone there, and he seemed special, somehow, when I met him. Doesn't take centuries on Earth to figure something like that out."

He studies his hands.

"Did Missy know?" she asks him again.

He shrugs. "I don't know. I don't know what she even thought about. It's such a pain to have to tell you so much all the time, but at least I always know where yer at in that head of yers. Missy was like a cloudy day. Sometimes a big storm."

"Figuring you out isn't rocket surgery."

"That's not the term."

"Brain science."

"Put those two things together."

"Rocket brain? Surgery science?"

"No!"

She gets it right and they both laugh.

They spend the next day riding the horses. The air is extremely cold despite the bright sunshine. Back at the house and chilled to the bone, Matt builds them a roaring fire.

They watch it for hours. As nighttime arrives, they don't even get up to turn on any lights. After a while, Missy turns from the fire and leans along the back of the couch once again, this time to look at the stars glistening in the sky.

"Why don't you just go live the life you were meant to live?" she finally asks.

Matt sighs. "Well, you know my dad fought in Viet Nam. His father fought in the second World War plus Korea. It was only right that my brother and I went off to fight in Afghanistan. But only one of us came home." He gets up to put another log on the fire. After he rejoins her on the sofa, he stares off into the distance, as well.

"Yes, you told me that."

"I couldn't let them lose two sons, both their children."

"They wouldn't lose both of you."

"If I ever told them, I'd lose them. They'd make sure of that."

"I think they deserve more credit than you're giving them. They can probably handle more than you think they can."

"Nah. One time I mentioned a gay guy. They then mentioned some friends who had a gay son and how they'd called in a minister to give him an exorcism." Matt explains the word to her.

"You're kidding me!"

"An abomination. That's what they say the church says."

"Jesus was about love. Isn't that what Christianity is supposed to be about?"

He ignores the question and looks at her. "I can't leave my parents, Missy. Can't do that to them."

"Then it's almost like you died, too."

He turns away.

She looks up at the expanse of stars. "See all those stars out there? That's what you're made of—stardust. You're made of the same stuff as those brilliant lights way out there. And you tell me you're not free to love whomever you want?"

He doesn't say anything for a few minutes, but when he speaks again it's with a smile. "How in creation do you know when to say whom, but you didn't know what an iPod is? Let alone a husband!"

"Don't change the subject."

"Yer like livin' with a real, live robot. Kinda strange. But then I have to tell you how robots, or at least gadgets, work."

Missy just smiles.

"My parents don't ask a lot of questions," Matt adds. "Neither did Missy. I could just go about my business."

"But you can't be who you really are."

"I'm who I am no matter who knows what about me. I know who I am." Matt sighs though. "I haven't even told you the worst part."

"What's that?"

"When I came back and Jason didn't, my father said to me, 'Shoulda been you.'"

Missy's jaw drops as tears sting her eyes. "Matt, why in all the cosmos are you so loyal to him, then?"

"And even worse than that? When he came back from Viet Nam and his brother didn't, his father said that very same thing to him."

"Oh my universe!"

"So you think he'da known how those words would land."

Missy takes his hand. They sit for a long while with just the crackles from the fire breaking the silence.

"I'm glad you came," Matt finally says.

"That's some pretty high praise, coming from you."

He chuckles. "What made you choose her and here?"

"I didn't choose her and here. We get sent wherever we're needed. Sometimes we're not sure why. I think I'm more unsure of why than most," she quips.

"Wisecracker."

"Do you miss her—I mean, now that you know she's not here?"

"I think I missed her more when she was here."

Missy's eyebrows come together as she thinks about his words. "She probably missed you, too," she says after a few minutes, "considering she really didn't know who you are. At all."

"Yep." He pauses. "But she mighta known."

"She okay?" he asks as they're getting ready for bed that night. "I mean, I do—I did—care about her."

"Yes, she's okay. More than okay. She's dead, but she's fine. Most who die are just fine—depends how they go out. This isn't the end all, be all of the universe."

"I think we both were calling it Hell not too long ago."

"It's also fabulous. It's a living, moving, breathing miracle. But it's not the only one."

"It's the only one I know of."

"You can go find your happy, you know."

They climb into bed. Matt turns away. Missy just lets him be in his quiet.

Crazy humans! Do you have any idea how big you are? You have the whole world. You have the whole of creation. And yet you insist on staying so very small.

CHAPTER 13

On Christmas Eve, after she requested his assistance, Matt pulls an outfit out of the closet for Missy to wear to church. The clothes hang on her once again.

"How much weight have, well, have Missy and I lost?"

"Oh, twenty-five pounds or so, I'd say."

As he guides her down the main aisle of the church, scores of people smile and wave at her.

"Welcome back, Missy."

"We prayed fer you, Missy."

"Missy, yer lookin' good. Yer sweet husband must be takin' mighty good care of you, huh?"

Missy and Matt sit next to her parents in the front row. As the preacher preaches, Missy feels like she's strangling.

After church, alone with him in the truck, she sighs. "Matt, you agree with all that stuff?"

"Not so much. But, like I say, it seems to keep people out of trouble. I went mostly because you—uh, Missy— liked to go, and it was a great way to see yer—uh, her— folks."

"I don't want to go. Would you be upset if we stop?"

"No. I think yer folks'll be sad if we stop, but we sure don't have to go."

Christmas seems to be a repeat of Thanksgiving—the same cast of characters, minus her brother and his family, and even all the food items. There's an extra plate of red meat, though, that has crisscrosses carved into it, with a dark, prickly thing stuck in the middle of each diamond shape. She obviously hasn't come across that particular food on Google yet.

"Want some ham, darling?" Linda asks as Missy hesitates in front of that offering.

"Sure."

She sits next to Matt on the sofa. "I never even asked you what your parents do on the holidays," she whispers to him.

"They go to Mom's sister over in Dodge City. You—well, Missy—and I used to try to do both but it just made fer a really crazy day."

"They don't mind not seeing you on Christmas?"

"We usually see them on New Year's."

Blech! The idea of spending time in that house for even just one minute makes Missy's skin crawl.

"They're not too crazy about yer parents ever since they switched churches and all," Matt explains.

"Why'd they switch? And why would your parents care?"

Matt shrugs. "Not really sure. Maybe just to have some high drama in their otherwise low-key lives."

Wackadoo humans. She'd read *wackadoo* on Google in the last few days and fell madly in love with it.

After she's a third of the way through with the heap of food once again, she stands to take her plate into the kitchen. Her uncle follows her. The hair on the back of Missy's neck prickles.

"You never, ever have to be within ten feet of me, ever again," she hisses.

He backs out of the kitchen. She can actually see his brain disconnecting as anger and guilt do a pas de deux (she was studying dance and metaphors on Google earlier that week, when perhaps she could have been studying food, especially holiday dinners). *Oh, wow. Being able to see that disconnection is new.*

As she walks back into the living room, she nearly has to stop to catch her breath. Around each human shines a ball of light with myriad colors shooting through it along with numerous images.

Ohhhhhhhhh! Here it is. Finally!

During her training for Earth, she'd been assured that she'd be able to see auras and fields around every humanoid. She was also to see the truth behind every statement, as humans tend to lie even more than they realize. Plus she was supposed to know about the lives of everyone around her as well as remember history, political science, names of things, the mechanics of how things work...and it all—*all*—suddenly came rushing in. She collapses onto the sofa.

"You okay?" Matt whispers. "You look like you've seen a ghost." And then as she blanches even more, he quickly adds, "It's just a saying we humans have here."

"I know," Missy breathes. "I think I'm seeing a lot of ghosts. I suddenly seem to know a lot of things."

She looks at the people around the room, and it's as though she's seeing television screens on top of television screens on top of more. Frank, even more than most of the others, has a highly active swirling sphere around him. She spies young soldiers in his realm. And...is that the dead toddler, the little girl Linda told her about?

Linda smiles at her, but Missy feels her pain. There's a strange man, about Linda's current age, showing up in a prominent position in her field. Missy has a visceral reaction to him.

Talk about Hell! She and Matt had been talking about the Hellishness of Earth even before she could see these spheres of Hell surrounding...everyone.

Leslie has a dark sphere around her, too. Missy suddenly realizes she doesn't want to know everything about everyone. If she has to know it for her Earth project, that's one thing. She quickly looks away from Leslie's sphere and avoids looking at anyone else's for the moment.

But even with looking away from the fields, the assault of the roomful of underlying emotions are way too much for her, and she feels queasy. The emotions seem to be layered in tiers: everyday irritations of getting through life—what with physical pains, complicated relationships, hard work, and financial concerns just to name a few—all the way down to the enormous tragedies that each and every person has to reckon with. Those seem to live in a crypt underneath their souls, hidden away, yet dictating their daily actions. This explains the slow, sludgy feeling that sometimes seems to hover over the planet.

At the same time, though, comes some underlying... what is it? Power? Grit? Beauty? All of the above?

It's like hearing the most beautiful symphony but with undertones of a requiem, with discordant, sharp notes. Or it's like that photo she saw online of an intrepid blade of grass growing between two slabs of a concrete sidewalk. Or perhaps it's like watching the most stunning, sublime sunset, but from a beehive. Such beauty and majesty...such friction and strain.

She gazes at the Christmas tree and see scallops of memories clinging to the ornaments. As she looks at one, she can see Linda and Missy in years gone by with tears slipping down their faces. Her eyes rest on Linda, and she has to catch her breath. The pain pulsating through her is palpable.

She looks over at Matt, beside her on the sofa. Such complexities live in this man. He's cloaked, though; she doesn't look at the thoughts or memories floating through his mind, but she can see the tumult of his inner turmoil and feel his pain.

Within Matt, Linda, and Frank, though, she can also feel their hope, the continuous yearning that life will deliver a better day. But in the kaleidoscope of optimistic expectations are the ever-present specks of being beaten down...but it's not just from their life experiences, Missy senses. There seems to be a circuit of...oh, what is it?

Lack? Fatigue? Apathy? This circuit seems to be circling the room, perhaps the planet.

And these two, Linda and Matt (not Frank, because of his war experiences)—as well as the others in the room—have a fairly decent life, an easier time than most on this planet. And still! The dashed dreams, the locked secrets move through the room like living beings.

She can't see the actual secrets, other than figures—such as the man, the toddler, and the soldiers—but she can feel the effect of them. The years wearing down the spark in the soul, the hunger in the heart growing and yet…it's quelled because there's no way for that hunger to be satiated, ever—at least as far as these folks know.

It seems to be like living in an upper chamber of a big house with sunshine pouring through skylights overhead, but with the chains and murkiness of the dungeon. *Owwwww.*

She glances over at Uncle Charlie, dreading what she'll find but still wanting to know. She doesn't shield herself from this sight…and there it is, right in his sphere: he took the innocence of a young Missy, perhaps thirteen or fourteen years old. She was quite mature for such a young age.

The current Missy sees self-assurance and confidence in the younger one. But this cowardly man attempted to steal them from her—he wanted that self-assurance and confidence for himself, to possess and feel those attributes inside, even more than he wanted to take her maidenhood. Disquiet reigned in his head, as he clearly didn't know that no one can steal those traits from another. She sees a gun held to Missy's head and a threat made, not just against her but against her family as well.

And yet…still in Charlie's sphere, she sees the young Missy shoulder this travesty and never tell another soul. *But why in creation would she ever work for him?*

She stares at Charlie until he nudges his wife and whispers to her, probably something along the lines of it being time to go.

"Already?" Jane asks. "We haven't even had dessert yet."

But he runs into Linda and Frank's bedroom to grab their coats from the stack on the bed.

"Charlie's not feeling too well," Jane says. "I need to get him home."

Charlie and Jane say their goodbyes to the group, with Charlie avoiding Missy's stare. Missy watches his complete disconnect. The truth sits in the center of the circle of his mind, but every time his thoughts come close, they quickly draw back as if brushing too near a fire.

After they leave, she looks at the star at the top of the Christmas tree. So much light, hope, expectancy, even optimism radiate from that star. So many secrets, agonies, hushed whispers, and tears come behind it.

"We finally got you reconnected," Bashiran tells her later that night.

"You don't say! Perhaps you could give me some warning next time? And what took you so long?"

"We were working on it! But you know three minutes in our world are like three weeks in this world."

"Are you sending me to Washington?"

"Well, hmmmmm, about that...now that you're here, you'll have to figure out how to get there."

"Great. Thanks. How about if I bilocate?"

"Nah, they don't take to that kind of thing so well."

"I can't stay here."

"You do seem to be doing fine."

"It hurts here, though."

"You think it'll be any better in Washington?"

"They live in so much pain," she sighs to him. "It's unbelievable how much they have inside of them, eating them up. And yet they're so big...and resilient...but still...."

"We don't come here because it's easy."

"Have you been here as a human?"

"Many times."

"I want your gig next time—help out without actually having to stay here. Like I said, it hurts."

"That's the beauty of it, really, if you think about it."

Great. I don't want to think about it.

Ann Crawford

CHAPTER 14

The next morning Linda calls to tell Missy that Charlie had a massive heart attack and died just after midnight.

"At least it wasn't on Christmas Day," she says through her sobs.

A strange man shows up in a pickup and walks down the pathway to the stable.

"Who's that?" Missy asks Matt.

"John. Something must've come up with Tommy."

Missy wanders down to the stable where John's feeding the horses. "Where's Tommy?" Missy asks him.

"He had to go home fer a while. His mom got real sick."

"Oh."

She saddles up Diamond Girl and heads to the fields, which are blurred by her tears.

When she's about halfway across the land, she spies Andy coming out of his little hut of a home. He then perches himself on the fence on the far end of the property, waiting. Missy decides to confront this particular situation.

"Whatever it was that we did together, I don't remember and I need to stay close to my husband," she says when she and Diamond Girl reach him.

"It's a lot to forget."

"Can you forget me?"

"Maybe. Maybe not." He smiles, again revealing the huge gaps between his few remaining teeth. The smile has no warmth to it at all.

What in the universe had Missy gotten herself into? Hey! She suddenly remembers she can look into his sphere. *Well, that's convenient.* She sees the old Missy and Andy doing drugs, sleeping together...and that's enough—she doesn't want to see any more. She leaves, much to Diamond Girl's joy. *With all the conflicts Missy was carrying, it's not much of a surprise that she'd try to deaden the pain.*

As she heads back to the stable, her heart sinks anew at the thought of not seeing Tommy. *When is he coming back?*

She laughs as her heart gives a little pang. One of the things starbeings laugh at from afar is how crazy stupid humans get when they fall into a crush or in love.

Oh, we have no idea. It might seem silly when viewed from far away, but it actually hurts. But not as much as it...oh...sizzles the soul...but it's a very good sizzle.

As Matt drives them to the funeral on the day before New Year's Eve, Missy thinks about Charlie—not only the life he lived here, but also the life he's headed to. What will that be? Again, the day reflects the color her heart feels: gray.

"The thing you humans don't seem to realize," she suddenly spouts out, "is that you never need to seek your own retribution or justice. Life does that for you. Life is an exacting taskmaster. I mean, you don't need to keep a known murderer or rapist on the street where he'll kill and rape more people, but even if you didn't put him away, life would catch up with him."

Matt remains quiet for several minutes as he recovers from his surprise over this statement, seemingly coming from nowhere, and then tries to digest it. "But if you left him out on the street, what about the people he hurts?" he asks. "What about the families who lose their loved ones?"

"What if that event is the event that makes them who they're supposed to be? I'm not justifying any bad actions or even making lemonade out of limes."

"Lemons."

"But what if the one most ghastly thing that happened in their lives makes them the superstars they were meant to be?"

Matt thinks about it. He's about to say something when Missy rushes on.

"That's where their pain comes from. It has to come from somewhere. There's no way around it here. It's how you beings crack open your hearts."

"Great. Shoulda been designed a little better."

"From far away, when we hear about all your human shenanigans, it sounds like Earth is just a crazy place, where people hurt each other for kicks or something. From up close, you people are the strongest beings I've ever met. It's easy for starbeings to be loving and gracious—we live forever in lands of love and peace and beauty. You do, too, but you have to look for it harder."

Matt thinks this over as well.

"Did you know Charlie raped Missy?"

Matt pulls over to the side of the road and is quiet for a few moments as he lets this information hit him in stages. "How did you find that out?"

"I saw it in his field on Christmas. I suddenly got my tracking powers."

"Great. What do you see in my field?"

"I don't look too much. I get to choose how much I want to see."

"In answer to yer question, I knew something happened to Missy. I just didn't know what."

They sit for a while longer.

"That's why we got along so well, I guess. We both had our deep, dark secrets and didn't bug the other about 'em. We were both just kind of live and let live with each other and pretty much left each other alone."

Missy nods.

"What about Les?" Matt asks.

"I'm not sure. I haven't really looked. I just saw what happened with Missy because it was so up in his field when he saw me. Actually, it wasn't—it was in the periphery in little bits...until I confronted him. And even then, it was crazy to watch his mind go into denial around it."

"Like I said, yer like living with a robot, or maybe a human-looking Siri or Alexa or something. Or maybe it's an emotional x-ray machine that you are."

Missy smiles.

"Good thing yer gettin' all yer Earth-walkin' practice with me," Matt says. "Like I said, big-city folks might not be as understanding of you or yer questions or yer photographic memory or yer ability to see people's past. Or a whole lotta things about you."

He puts the pickup back in gear and slowly heads down the snowy road to the church.

At the funeral, Missy tries to avoid gazing into Les's sphere too much. But there's no avoiding Les at the reception.

"Oh, Missy," she cries, "I'm so happy we all got to see him on Christmas, at his best, one last time."

With that, Missy stops avoiding her sphere. But there's nothing in there anywhere close to what happened to the former Missy—and for that the present Missy is grateful.

On New Year's Day, as she and Matt sit in his parents' home, Missy pulls a shield around her. Their pain, too, is palpable. It's settled into the straight line of his mother's mouth, but Missy can see her mouth is set that way to keep from screaming or bursting into tears or... something.

She sees snippets of the past in both Bart and Rita's fields, but she doesn't pry too much. Her heart aches for these fragile human creatures. Fragile, but with structures of steel. Soft insides under masks of hardened clay. Delicate sand castles built on fortresses of rock.

Even the aching of her heart feels good, though. It means she cares....well, as a starbeing she always cares. But elsewhere the beings don't have this human sense, this ache. It doesn't hurt as much as it's a... privilege.

Her in-laws have the television running in the background, and the news program has a segment on the President. Missy's eyes go wide as she sees his thoughts jumping over each other—swirling, avoiding, diving, flailing. It's like watching an exhausted, near-drowning swimmer surfacing and returning to the same buoy over and over, but the buoy is broken.

She knows his diet consists of fast food and diet soda, which isn't real nutrition. She can see his brain disconnecting.

"He's not...real," she whispers to herself. "Just like his food. Just like his words. Just like his marriage."

Watching his disconnection and trying to cling to the broken buoy is physically painful.

Owwwwwww. That guy is in some serious pain. And he's lashing out and inflicting it on as many people as he can.

"That poor man," Rita says. "He's under such an assault from the Left. They never cut him any slack."

"Mmmmmmmmm," Missy responds.

She tries to follow the President's words some more. He's actually quite brilliant but deeply, deeply troubled in his soul. The crazy back and forth is, well, crazy-making to her.

It's like dancing with a squid, to hear him talk.

"They're so...fascinating," she says to Bashiran that night. "So strong. So weak. It's such a wild mix of things—of the best and worst of life in any of the universes." She sighs. "Some of this misery is of their own making. But a lot just comes their way. She didn't ask for her baby or her grown son to die. Those events broke her heart."

"But her journey is about healing her broken heart, not sitting in it for her whole lifetime."

"But right now she's living in a prison." Missy pauses. "Of her own making, though, I suppose."

"And?" Bashiran asks.

"I guess it's up to her to figure out how to get herself out of it. One thing I'm learning quickly is you can't tell these human creatures anything. They have to come to the idea of their volition."

"That's for sure."

"And I have to figure out how to get myself to Washington. That man is under a spell, and so is a big chunk of this country."

"Any ideas on how you're going to do that?"

"Not really, other than relying on Leslie somehow."

But I'll get there.

"Yes, you will," her mentor says. "Nice try. Have you already forgotten that we hear everything?"

CHAPTER 15

The endless white fields have turned to green. Flower blossoms cover the fruit trees that dot the yard.

As the rays of the sun peek over the edge of forever, Missy sees luminous light coming from inside these living flowers—unlike with the cut flowers way back in her hospital room or the ones she sees in the grocery store. The sun rises a little higher, illuminating the cobwebs in the tall grasses and causing the drips of dew to sparkle like jewels.

She absentmindedly pushes herself back and forth in the porch swing, mesmerized by the scene. A meadowlark sings.

Matt joins her on the porch.

"It's not so bad here," she smiles.

"Told you."

"Just have to wait until spring."

"Yep. But I like winter, too. Just give me a season—I like 'em all."

She moves from the swing to perch on the railing. "I saw the flowers in the neighbor's yard. I might want to get something like that going."

"Missy, you think you'll be able to go back to work anytime soon? I mean, if yer fully up and running now, can you find some work to do? The insurance money is about to run out."

"What would I do?"

"Anything. Most people around here—meaning on Earth—have to do something fer a living. You could go back to the feed barn, especially now that Charlie's gone. The old Missy never liked it there."

"Now you know why."

"Why in creation would she have worked there, considering all he did to her?"

Missy had been thinking about that a great deal. "I think she stole from him, to try to make up for what he stole from her, and otherwise made his life miserable there," she says.

"Yep, sounds like something Missy'd do."

"Of course it didn't work...in fact it had the opposite effect, as actions like that tend to do."

Matt contemplates her words for a couple of minutes. "Well," he finally says, "you gotta do somethin'. I mean, it'd be one thing if yer raising a family."

"Maybe I can do that."

He does a double take. "Missy never could."

"I'm not Missy. Well, not entirely, anyway."

"What're you sayin'?"

She doesn't answer, just smiles.

"Are you sayin'—" his voice breaks off.

"Yes, I'm saying that," she says.

Matt looks out at the fields. "I don't know what to say. I mean, what kind of being will it be?"

"It'll be human. I'm in a human body. You're human. Together that makes a human baby."

"We haven't done anything since that one time we actually did it."

"We actually did it more than once, thank you for remembering so well. And it only takes once."

"But the human body you're in wasn't able to make a baby."

"Well, it can now. Things change."

"I thought you were just gaining Missy's old weight back," he laughs, except not really. "Well, that's really... great."

His eyes tell a completely different story from his words. She thought he would've been much happier.

Doesn't every human want to be a parent? Or at least most of them?

"You're not happy. Didn't you ever want to be a father?"

"Yeah. Sure."

"I believe you. A quadrillion starbeings wouldn't believe you, but I believe you," she teases.

Matt examines his hands—something he loves to do when he doesn't want to talk, she's noticed over the months.

"I'll take care of him or her," she tells him. "You can go to Denver every weekend for all I care."

"Well, I'll need to get another job, maybe. We'll see. You been to a doctor?"

She nods.

"Well, that's good, anyway." He wanders off toward the stable.

Back in January she and Matt bought a new car with the insurance money, and he taught her to drive. She instantly picked it up, and he almost as quickly came to regret teaching her...because that meant she could go grocery shopping on her own.

On her first solo grocery-store trek, Missy meandered through the store, not wanting to put any of the food (fake, as she considered it) into her shopping cart. She Googled health-food store on her phone and found one... in the same town that has the siren's coffee place. As she leaves the fake-food store, she again notices the tabloids shouting their bogus headlines. As before, she's struck by the odd juxtaposition.

Selling lies with lying food. No wonder so many of them have indigestion.

Later that day Matt walked in to the kitchen to find her sipping a very goopy green...goop. "Missy, what the hell?"

"More like what the heaven. It's spirulina, along with blueberries, cacao, flax milk, and some other things.

Want some?" She took another sip of her delicious delight.

"Uhhhhh, no, that's alright. Thanks anyway."

She'd also taken herself to Starbucks and Matt spied the cup. "Why are you drinking goop after drinking yer million-calorie car'mul thing?"

"Why do you say car'mul when it's spelled *caramel*? Why do you say Dor'thy when it's spelled *Dorothy* and both are pronounced the way they're spelled? Unlike a lot of this crazy language. Let alone t'al for *towel*. And not to mention *syrup* is two syllables, not s'urp. And *ornery* is or-ne-ry, not on'ry."

"We're syllable poor around here," Matt chuckles. "But answer my question. If yer going to drink a venti cup of sugar, why bother drinking goop?"

"You can have a treat once in a while." She took a sip of her other delicious delight.

The last time Missy saw Linda and Frank was about a month ago. As she drove herself over to their house, she thought about how much she loves to consider them her parents. She tries not to see the fields around them too much—it feels like prying. The last visit, though, she noticed the man in Linda's field was quite visible. He still made her stomach turn. She also noticed that he was in a churchlike building, perhaps standing at a pulpit. And was there another man in a similar setting? She'd gotten most of her starbeing sight powers going on Christmas, but some of the details remain a mystery.

"Momma, did something happen with a man in a church?" she asked.

Linda's eyes widened. "Something did, honey." She paused. "The pastor of our former church had touched you inappropriately when you were a teenager." She wiped away a tear. "We didn't want to believe you, and fer that I'm so sorry. We changed churches, which is a big deal in a small town like ours." She paused again.

"Same thing happened to me when I was young, so you'da thought I woulda believed you faster."

"Wow!" The number of multi-generational traumas in both her and Matt's families struck Missy as odd...and sad. "I'm sorry that happened to both of us."

Linda took her hand.

"Why didn't you sue him?" Missy asked, thinking of all the news about priests being accused of sexual misconduct.

"Our churches don't have deep pockets like the Catholics do. The priests definitely don't have the market on abuse; that's all over the place. It's just that our churches are independent entities, not part of the richest organization on Earth. Plus in our world, it's always the woman's fault...even if she's only sixteen. Or younger."

"Why do you stay a member of such a place, even if you do go to another, uh, branch?"

Linda shrugged. "Habit, I guess. I've been going to church since I was a babe in arms. It's what I do. I don't know what I'd do in its place. But that's why all the others—other than Catholics—keep so quiet about it. I mean, talking about it'd be the right thing to do, but it wouldn't get us very far."

"You can't just let him stay in that position and possibly do it to others. What kind of a world is this where people just help themselves to other people's bodies or other people's belongings or even their spirits?"

The look on Linda's face told her to stop while she was ahead.

During that visit she also found out more about the toddler in Frank's field. He'd been hiding in the bushes with his platoon in Viet Nam, and someone from the nearby village threw a grenade at them. The young men fired back. The two-year-old fell to the ground—and Frank was closest to her. Her mother came out of her little home screaming and tearing her clothing, as Linda had said.

"Can't say fer sure it was me," he told Missy. "But most likely it was, just given her proximity." He'd also been exposed to Agent Orange (which Missy Googled later that night), hence his need for oxygen.

On that visit Linda told her about her several miscarriages she'd had before and after both Rod and Missy's births. "I don't know why I never told you about them," Linda said, eyes glistening. "I still try to picture what they'd look like now, had they lived. I'm beyond grateful for you and your brother...but I do miss them so much."

Missy's heart softened and her compassion grew exponentially on that visit. *Oh, the endless pain these people have to endure.*

On this beautiful May day, she drives herself over to her parents again. For a while, just wearing the old Missy' old clothes, she could hide her stomach.

Linda waves from the front porch. But as Missy emerges from the car, Linda's eyes widen.

"Yes, Momma, I'm pregnant."

Linda's eyes register shock and then fill with tears. "Baby girl," she whispers, then puts a hand over her mouth.

"Momma, aren't you happy?"

"Of course I'm happy. Those are words I wanted to hear fer so long from you and never thought I would." They sit on the porch swing.

"But...you don't seem as happy as you say."

Linda stares at her for a long while. "Yer not her. Yer not my baby." She bursts into tears.

Missy just sits by her side, letting her cry. Finally, when the tears slow, she takes Linda's hand. "I'm not going to insult you by pretending anymore. If you know, you know. But how did you know?"

"Well, first of all, I'm the one who took Missy to doctor after doctor after doctor—all over these parts, and then to Wichita, and then as far away as Kansas City, trying to figure out why she couldn't have a baby."

Missy'd had a flash about the old Missy....It might've been easier to let her mother take her all over creation to have her insides checked out than to tell her that her husband didn't want to have sex with her, or at least not more than once a year. Missy'd never read the reports to her mom that told her she was perfectly healthy.

"Things can change," Missy replies. "Bodies can suddenly start working the way they're supposed to."

"Yeah, but nah. It's not just that. I had Missy in my womb. I knew her her whole life. There was an energy in the room when she was around. You have a different energy. It's a fine energy, sure, but it's not hers. I knew almost right away."

The tears flow again and Missy continues to just sit with her.

"I'm happy about the baby," Linda finally says. "But where's my baby?"

Missy doesn't respond.

"Did she go to Hell?"

"Hell? There is no Hell. Only the one you humans love to put yourselves in while you're here. But if there was such place as Hell, why would you think she ended up there?"

"She...got...well...kinda confused. She got involved with someone she shouldn't have."

"Andy?"

Linda nods. "He got her into drugs and stuff. I don't know why. I don't know why Matt wasn't enough fer her."

Missy sighs. She starts to say something and then changes her mind.

Linda grabs her arm. "Where'd she go? Where'd my baby go?"

"To whatever comes next after this."

Linda bursts into tears again.

"Missy is fine, Momma."

"Don't call me that! You are not my child, so don't call me that!"

Missy is silent.

"I'm sorry," Linda says through her tears. "I thought I was losing her in the hospital, and then she came back to me. But it wasn't her. I knew, but I didn't let on that I knew—even to myself. That make sense?"

Missy nods.

"My heart is breaking all over again, worse than back when I thought she was dying. I understand dying. I don't understand you!" She runs into the house, the screen door slamming behind her.

Missy returns home and wanders down to the stable. She nuzzles her forehead into Diamond Girl's muzzle, one of her favorite things to do.

"Hey there, Miss," calls a familiar voice from the doorway.

"Tommy!"

"How ya been? Actually, from the looks of things, ya been great. How far along are you?" He flashes a smile, revealing those dimples that do that thing to her heart.

"Just over five months."

"Congrats."

She smiles, but only with her lips, not her heart. "Thank you, Tommy. Where've you been?"

"My mom took sick."

"Is she better now?"

"Yep. Fer a bit, anyway."

Tommy saddles up Mystery and heads toward the door. He stops the horse and looks back at her. "The answer's yes." His smile does another encore of flashing those dastardly dimples that melt—*yeah, that's what it does*—her heart.

That is so not fair.

"To what question?"

"The one in yer eyes. If the circumstances were different, yes."

She's too surprised to say anything. After he leaves, she buries her face in Diamond Girl's mane once again. *Those circumstances certainly can be different.* "I'll tell him that tomorrow," she says to the horse's very sympathetic eyes.

But he doesn't come back the next day, or the next. She guesses his mom took another turn.

A few days later, back in Matt's parents' hovel, as Missy prefers to think of it, her body is on high alert. *Actually, that's an insult to hovels. At least hovels have some semblance of a loving home sometimes. It's absolutely amazing Matt turned out as well as he did.*

As always, the television is on, blasting the news from a station that seems to prefer making incendiary remarks.

"The officer involved in the killing of a young black man was sentenced today," the petite blonde newscaster reports with a strange smile plastered onto her face.

Missy isn't sure, but she might've heard a racial slur in a comment Bart mutters. The news switches to a story about a Muslim man.

"They should go to church," Rita states. "Not that mosque thing they go to."

"You know," Missy says, ignoring Matt's eyes widening at the fear of whatever she's going to say and whatever trouble it's going to lead into with his parents, "all religions are based on their own interesting creation story." She elaborates on Dreamtime, Shiva and Parvati, and the many others she studied so many months before.

"Well, they're wrong." Rita crosses her arms.

"They think you're wrong," Missy says.

"Well, they're wrong again." Bart punctuates his statement with a burp.

"Let's talk about something else." Rita turns down the sound on the television. "Matt, yer cousin needs yer prayers. She's quite sick."

"What do you want him to pray for?" Missy asks. Matt looks like he wants to dive under the table...if it wasn't so scary down there on the floor, that is.

"That she gets better, of course." Rita's obviously out of patience and wondering where her old daughter-in-law went.

But Missy's on a roll. "What if that disease, or whatever she has, is exactly what she needs to heal something else in her soul? Or what if her death leads her husband to marry someone else and the child they have becomes the next Martin Luther King or Gandhi or Jesus?"

"There's only one Jesus!"

"There's only one of any of us, but you get my point." Missy spots a homeless man on the news. "What if that homelessness is exactly what he needs?"

"Yer not blaming the victim, are you?" Bart asks.

Missy's stunned he even knows that phrase. "No, I'm empowering him as a master creator of his own destiny. It doesn't mean we shouldn't help him. But what if that horrible event is exactly what that person needs to become the person he or she was meant to be—a radiant, bright light in a sea of darkness?"

Her in-laws stare at her in stunned silence.

"Maybe we should go," Matt says.

Out in the car, Matt just sits with raised eyebrows, tapping his fingers one at a time in quick sequence on the steering wheel.

"I'm not sorry," Missy says.

Matt continues to tap. Missy squares her shoulders.

"It's not a bad thing to make us unwelcome there," she says. "You want to know what Hell looks like? It's what they're living in—all that hate and judgment, let alone the filth they surround themselves with. It all comes back to them, too: they're living in the very hate and judgment that they're creating."

Matt starts the car and they drive home in silence. But Missy notices that he doesn't look upset; he looks more...relieved.

As Missy and Matt sit in the porch swing close to sunset, Linda drives up to the house.

"Make yerself at home," Matt says to her, standing up as she arrives at the porch. "I gotta check on the horses." He heads down the pathway to the stable.

Linda sits in a chair next to the swing. Missy watches her as she gathers her thoughts and starts to speak several times.

"Frank doesn't have to know," she finally says.

"No. He doesn't."

"We don't have to go breakin' his heart all over again."

"No. We don't."

"He's seen enough action fer one lifetime, and I don't mean figuratively."

"Yes."

Linda stares out at the setting sun for a long while. "How many of you are there?" she asks quietly.

"Millions. All over Earth. Not just as humans, by the way."

"What did you come here for? What did you want to tell us?"

"I came here to help. But I wasn't supposed to be sent here." Missy stops abruptly as a wail erupts from Linda's throat. No—the wail comes from her heart.

"You weren't supposed to be here? You took over my baby and you weren't even supposed to be here?"

"Missy was dying anyway. It's not like I took her life or anything. And, yes, I was supposed to be somewhere else—one of the best friends of the President's family."

Linda gasps. "What was supposed to happen to her?"

"She was supposed to die in a car accident. Something happened at the last minute, so she wasn't killed,

129

she didn't die. But at that moment Missy did. And I got shifted over here."

Linda remains silent, trying to grasp what Missy's telling her.

"I'd had eons of training in politics, diplomacy, life in Washington, even espionage, that whole thing. I didn't have any training on Kansas or horses or cattle or farms or meth. But I lost practically everything—all my training in life on Earth—in the shift anyway, except how to speak and read some English."

Linda digests this for a few minutes. Then she just gives a long, "Hmmmmmm."

Missy stares out across the fields. "The sun looks quite halcyon."

"Halcyon?"

"It means golden."

"I know. You can just say golden. Halcyon implies more than just golden," Linda laughs.

"When you see this word how do you decide what it means? Why don't they just come up with more words and just have halcyon mean happy and golden?"

Linda shrugs. "You might have a photographic memory, or whatever, to remember all this stuff you've been studying, but you haven't been given the logic of when to use what. It's kind of endearing."

A month later, the two women amble through Linda's garden as the sun sets over the fields of wheat, turning the golden hue of the crop a darker shade of amber. The combines are at the ready to start cutting for harvest the next day. The small windmill creaks as it slowly spins in the warm, lazy breeze.

Linda's garden is a masterpiece of visual and aromatic beauty. The pungent perfume comes primarily from her rose bushes, hyacinths, rosemary, mint, sage, and basil. Behind the flower garden lies a large vegetable patch with a cornucopia of produce: lettuce, cucumbers, peppers, carrots, celery. It's a living salad.

"What about...." Linda stops. Missy patiently gives her the time and space to come up with the words—and doesn't look in her sphere for a preview. Linda sighs. "When people die, they often don't go away. They hang around. I felt my mother with me fer years. Still do."

"Yes."

"But when you people—beings—come in, the folks who've died might be hanging around but we don't know that."

"Because you're not supposed to know we're not your loved one," Missy responds.

"Right. So what happens? How can the being communicate with us if we don't know he or she is gone?"

"Well, how can you miss someone you don't know is gone? Most folks think they're still talking to their loved ones."

Linda shakes her head at the complexity of it all. "But that's not real. We don't really know who we're talking to. It's kind of a lie. And we have absolutely no idea that it's a lie."

"But we don't come here for bad reasons. We come because there's an opportunity to help. We're not trying to take anything away from you."

Linda doesn't respond.

"Besides, your Missy is right next to you. Tell her whatever you want. And now that you know she's there, you might hear her responses."

Missy exits the garden to allow Linda to start a whole new conversation.

As Missy drives through the little town, she smiles. *It's not so bad here. It's peaceful, mostly. There's work to do here, too, I guess. Maybe I can just stay here. After all, I have a baby to take care of now.*

She doesn't even see the huge pickup about to T-bone her car.

CHAPTER 16

"She's wakin' up again!"

"Missy, you comin' back to us?"

"Darling, yer awake! Are you alright?"

Missy slowly flutters her eyes open. Matt, Linda, and Frank hover over her, their faces revealing relief but afraid to show too much hope yet.

"Can you talk, sweetheart?" Linda asks.

"Haven't I been here before?" Missy asks. "Didn't I already go through this? What happened? Oh—no!" She puts her hand on her belly and looks up at Matt and her parents.

"You lost the baby, honey," Matt says.

"That drunken idiot made sure of that," Linda says through her tears. She clenches her fists to keep from bursting into sobs.

Frank starts to speak. Instead, he makes that sound he tends to make, deep in his throat, when the pain blocks his words.

Burning hot tears form in her eyes and slip down her face. The pain in her heart is unspeakable and she can barely breathe. Wasn't she thinking not so long ago that the pain humans feel is a privilege?

Perhaps it still is, even when it's excruciatingly unbearable. Perhaps when it's excruciatingly unbearable, it's even more so. Maybe that's what makes it bearable. Somewhat.

Her family had stayed with her in turns again, but she's alone for a spell while Matt takes a trip to the store and Starbucks to gather some of her favorite foods. She stares out the window. At least the endless fields aren't covered with snow now; the green and gold extend far off into the dusty distance.

Sights and sounds and sensations flash through her mind: The high pitch of tires squealing. Metal crashing into metal. Her car being pushed across an intersection and into another car. More metal crashing into metal and glass smashing. Flashing red lights. Some kind of contraption with metal plates breaking open the roof of the car. Being lifted out and gently placed on a stretcher and into the waiting ambulance.

Was this the former Missy's accident or her own? Or both? What are the chances of an accident like that repeating itself?

Liz, the nurse from her earlier sojourn in the hospital, enters her room. "You must be part cat—you definitely have nine lives. At least yer starting yer third. And you don't have amnesia this time. I've never had anyone enjoy rediscovering the bathroom the way you did."

Missy laughs. "Everything seemed totally brand new then. It was really fun. Well, mostly."

"How long did it take you to get yer memory back?"

"Oh, not too long," Missy answers. "Sometimes I still wonder about it."

"You and all of us," Liz cracks.

Once again, Missy convalesces at her parents. Matt had gone to Denver as soon as Missy woke up from the second accident, at her insistence.

"You just lost a baby and were in yer second major car accident in under a year. Well, kind of. At least the body you're in had two. I can't exactly pack up the pickup and leave."

"Sure you can. I want you to. Go."

So she and Linda sit, slowly pushing the porch swing with their legs in synchronized languor.

Missy gazes at a sunflower peeking over the railing at her. Like a green hand of love, the outer petals hold the flare of yellow petals, which surround the soft yellow-brown pad. She loves how the center is textured, nubbly even, like special parts of some pieces of Linda's needlepoint. She runs her finger along the fuzzy stalk. She thrills in all the aspects of this piece of Creation's handiwork as she did when she first laid eyes on those sunflowers in the hospital so many months ago. Light emanates from within this flower, however.

As Missy studies this universe in miniature before her, a butterfly softly lands on the flower. Magic bumps his snout into her leg for a pet and she complies.

"Toto, I have a feeling I'm back in Kansas," she smiles at him.

Linda snorts and laughs. And laughs. And laughs. Missy starts to become alarmed when the laughing doesn't stop.

"Momma, you alright?"

"Oh my goodness, that's the funniest thing I've ever heard!" Linda starts a whole new round of chortles interspersed with snorts and snickers.

When Missy is sure her Earth mother has not taken leave of her senses, she returns to examining the flowers. Her hands still pet Magic, catapulting him into bliss. The smell of freshly mowed grass hangs in the mugginess of the early-evening air.

"I wonder if grass minds being mowed."

"You are the most interesting thing," Linda giggles. "Ever."

They listen to the meadowlarks' song.

"Ever wonder what they're sayin'?" Linda asks.

"I think they're just sayin' they're happy to be here."

As the sun sinks lower in the sky, the cicadas join in with their song.

"It's such a symphony here."

135

"This certainly seems to be our time of day," Linda says, taking Missy's hand.

Missy lets out a long, long sigh. She wanted the baby. She wants this life. And she senses that with this second accident Linda has realized she wants this being in her life, even if she isn't her daughter. She's another daughter—a stardaughter.

"Family is by choice, sometimes," Missy says, taking Linda's hand in both of hers, much to Magic's dismay.

"Yes," Linda responds, holding her hand more tightly. "What's it like where yer from?"

"Easier in a million ways. But we don't have the comparisons, the highs and lows. We don't have bodies, so we don't have physical pain. But we don't have love the way you have it. For us, everything is love, which is great. But there's no dark to the light of love so we don't know what's missing.

"We watch what you do on this planet and think, 'Why don't they just get their act together?' We have no idea how much you deal with, what the pain in the heart feels like. How complicated it is to try to work with nine billion different opinions.

"We think we could run it so much better. But we can't. 'Why can't you just live like us,' we'd wonder. It's because you're not supposed to. You're the ones in the bodies, in the physical bodies. You have so much more, in a way.

"We can be on the other side of the universes with just a thought. You have to grow up for eighteen years, learn to drive, feed yourself every day and make sure you get enough rest and exercise.

"And then your loved ones die. Other people violate you. And you have wars that scar your soldiers for life. And then some of you carry that pain and trauma into the next lifetime, and the next, and the next."

Linda remains quiet, as Missy is obviously on a spree with her long-quiet thoughts now being given a voice.

"But you keep righting yourselves. You keep steering the ship. No matter how hard it gets, most of you just keep on going and going. You live in cars and under bridges, yet still get up every day. You have droughts and pestilence that take your crops. And yet you plant again. You have natural disasters that level your towns. And yet you build again.

"You have family members who steal from you—not only material things but also your joy, your innocence. And yet you still love them, you still forgive them, you still feed them if they're hungry, you still give them the shirt off your back.

"You have people ruining your food and your air and your water. Other countries have leaders who keep the food from the starving people. And yet you develop new ways to get food and water.

"You have people who kill your brethren. You have communities under constant siege. Some of you live alone with no touch and no conversation. And yet you keep on going. You keep on singing and dancing and loving and being awed by the vastness of space. You make new discoveries on top of new discoveries—time after time. Does that all make sense?"

Linda nods, obviously struck silent by Missy's flow of words. The sun has set by now, casting orange and pink light on the clouds.

"And you have that!" Missy says, pointing to the sky. "And you have this," she says, gesturing to her Earth mother's hand in hers.

Morning finds the two women slowly swinging in the porch swing again, watching the sunrise as well as the steam rising from their coffee cups.

"Did you ever want more than this?" Missy queries.

"Not really," Linda says. "What could be more than living on the land, off the land?"

"There's a whole lot to see out there."

"They can have it. I'm happy right here."

"And you lift up the world just by being here, just by being who you are, right here in this spot, being your happy you."

Linda smiles through the tears forming in her eyes. "What a wild life we have. So much loss. So much gain. Like you."

Leslie comes by the house for a visit while she's home helping her mother settle her father's affairs. Missy longs to know if Charlie had hurt her, too—so she asks her, outright.

"No. I mean, he wasn't the best father ever, but he never physically hurt me." She's quiet for a minute. "Why do you ask?" Missy doesn't answer. "Did he hurt you?" She receives her answer by Missy's silence. "Oh my God, I think I'm going to be sick." She fights back tears. "I'm so sorry," she whispers.

They sit in a long silence as Leslie absorbs the new information. "Is that why you married a gay man?" she finally asks.

Missy gasps. "How did you know that? Does everyone know?"

Leslie shrugs. "I doubt it. I'm probably the only one. I somehow knew you wanted to be with a guy like Matt, someone who wouldn't make too many demands on you. I just never knew why. And I never knew why he didn't just leave and go create another life for himself."

"So much for having secrets. Everyone knows every-thing anyway."

"I didn't know the one you kept about my dad. I'm so sorry that happened to you."

The two sit in a long silence again, both lost in their thoughts.

"I've been thinking of moving," Missy finally says. "Your way, that is. I don't think I can go through another winter here."

"D.C. isn't much better, you know."

"Can't be worse."

"By the way," Leslie says, pulling her phone from her purse, "here's a video of Roberta Doyle. I remember you were interested in her. There aren't many pictures or videos of her for some reason."

The video shows Roberta signing a card while the President and his family stand nearby, back in the early days of his presidency.

"She's left-handed."

"Uh-huh. So?"

"Nothing." *Just that seems to be the only thing that remains of me coming in to be her.*

Missy returns to the little house a day before Matt's scheduled homecoming from Denver. But she's not alone for long. A face appears in the window and she screams. She quickly recognizes him, though.

"Andy! Oh my galaxy! What in creation are you doing? You scared the living life out of me!"

Andy opens the kitchen door, which she hadn't locked yet. "Do you remember yet, Missy Miss?"

Missy freezes at his tone and entrance with no invitation. "Remember what? Did you know I was just in the hospital again?"

"You look in good shape to me. How's that faggot husband of yers?"

"Matt's fine. I'm the one who just got out of the hospital."

"Like I said, you look good to me. You always did, even when you was doin' all those drugs I gave you. You've cost me so much money. It's payback time." He moves toward her, top speed.

Starbeings might stumble around in this third-dimensional world at times, but when they have to, all their training, strength, and reflexes can kick into high gear. Accident? What accident? Missy takes the motion of Andy's forward propulsion toward her and flips him over her back—surprising herself even more than him.

"What the fuck, Miss!"

He starts to get up off the floor and she slams her foot onto his neck. He's not a very big man, thankfully. She probably could've done the Aikido move with a bigger man, but probably not the foot-on-the-neck move. Plus, Andy's fumbling moves from his years of drug use give her an advantage.

But he grabs her by the knee, knocking her to the floor. He comes at her again, but again she uses his forward motion to keep him going over her head, crashing onto the floor again.

Another face appears in the window.

"What is this, Grand Central Space Station?" she asks Tommy, nearly bursting into tears at the sight of him.

"Missy, you alright? I was out in the fields and saw Andy headin' to the house. Not a great sight to see."

Andy tries once more to get up until his neck meets Missy's foot again.

Tommy calls 911 and waits with Missy while Andy sprawls on the kitchen floor, not even looking up at them. After the police come and go, with Andy in the back of the patrol car and a restraining order in the works, Tommy turns to her.

"Where you been and what happened?"

"Hospital. Another accident."

He starts to look at her belly, but stops himself. She's wearing very baggy clothes anyway, so not much would be revealed. "And the baby?"

She shakes her head, pushing back her tears.

"I'm so sorry, Miss. Really I am." He puts on his cowboy hat. "I gotta go. Lock it behind me."

What in the Milky Way?

It's very uncharacteristic of Tommy to hear bad news and then just bolt like that. Long after he leaves, she stares at the door he gently closed behind him.

The next day, as she's paying a visit to the mailbox out by the road, a car stops.

"Can you tell me where the Floyd house is?" asks the woman who emerges from the vehicle.

Strangers on this road are a rarity. And something about this woman didn't seem like a stranger. Missy removes her sunglasses and the woman does the same. A glint, like with Shamaeya back at the motel, flashes from her eyes.

"Where are you from?" Missy asks, smiling through her tears.

The being waves her hands in a strange way—kind of like a cross between hula and belly dancing.

"OMG, that's so Nebula Galaxy," Missy giggles.

The other being laughs. "You got it! My name's Alia— my short name, anyway. Some of us from this region are going around to try to gather us together for a, well, a gathering."

"Gathering us together for a gathering. That sounds good. Where and when? And how did you know I was here and now?"

They laugh. Alia admires the expanse of the fields, the birds singing, the butterflies playing among the fruit trees.

"You got a nice quiet one, that's for sure."

"Not as quiet as it might seem. Lots of rumblings underneath everyone. Crazy people in huts. Drugs all over the place. Sexual assault. Life-diminishing lies. Post-traumatic stress disorder in so many people."

"It's crazy all over this planet. As crazy as it's beautiful."

"Yes. So where are we meeting? When?"

"Grand Tetons. Late October. Think you can get there?"

Missy shrugs. "I'll do my best." Although she sees Bashiran fairly frequently and calls and texts Shamaeya often, she misses her beings. "Why don't they just give us the information in the sleep space, when we talk to our mentors? Not that it's not great to see you."

"And make me miss out on driving through Kansas?" Alia laughs.

A week later, Missy and Matt go to see her relatives in Greensburg for her cousin's wedding.

"You sure yer up fer a small trip and a visit with a tractorful, plus twelve, of extended family? You've been through a lot in the last month. I'm amazed yer even up and walking as well as you are. And that incident with Andy didn't help anything."

"I'm fine."

As her aunt had told her at Thanksgiving, Greensburg had been completely wiped out by a tornado several years prior. No one died, though, as she had mentioned, because the town had plenty of advance warning. And it was completely rebuilt—green!

Very appropriate, considering its name.

Her numerous cousins are in full force. Yet another table is laden with an array of interesting foods, includeing a bowl with small white squares in a jiggly mass of orange. Missy hasn't come across that one on Google. Very sweet. She recognizes watermelon from her sojourns to the grocery store. This particular watermelon is cut into the shape of a shark with an open mouth, and its insides are filled with blueberries, grapes, strawberries, as well as scoops of the watermelon's innards.

"Oh, yes, that's where the tornado got us," Aunt Flo laughs, pointing to a small gash in the table by Missy's plate.

Missy's jaw drops as her aunt relays the amazing story how every one of the buildings in the town was leveled...yet some of the furniture and even some plates and glasses made it through the tornado unscathed.

Missy notices that as they're leaving, Matt's goodbyes are far more heartfelt than he usually shows.

She stares out the window on the drive home. "My aunt is happy—genuinely happy that is. Not this face that you humans usually put on."

"Mmmmmmmmm," was Matt's only response. They drive the rest of the way home in silence. But it's full of communication.

"Bashiran," Missy says to him that night, "this is a good life here. It's a little too interesting in spots here and there, that's for sure. But, as I keep telling you, I was supposed to come into a much bigger project."

"It's up to you. There's plenty of work to do here, too, as you know."

"It's not so bad here. Except when it is."

"Maybe just go to Washington a few times to get the lay of the land, as humans like to say. You can work from here once you have a better idea what to do."

"What about...."

"What about what?"

"Nothin'. Great, now I'm starting to sound like them."

"That's not a bad thing. Especially since you live here with them."

What about....? She doesn't even want to think his name.

Ann Crawford

CHAPTER 17

Missy stares out the kitchen window as she washes the breakfast dishes, mesmerized by the fall foliage and relishing the coolness of the air coming in through the open window. The splashes of color on the trees stand in stark contrast to the dry, sundrenched fields. Matt walks in the back door and reaches for the coffee pot.

"Matt, why don't you just go live in Denver?" Missy asks. "Your parents will get over it. Or they won't. Their choice. Meanwhile, you have a life to live."

He's quiet for several minutes. "What'll you do?"

Her eyebrows go up at his words, which convey that he's not averse to the idea and obviously had been thinking about it himself. *Thus those heartfelt goodbyes in Greensburg.* "I might just go see what I can do in Washington," she says.

"What about Tommy?"

She's barely even surprised at the question and the knowledge it communicates—she laughs and rolls her eyes. "I am sure not very good at keeping secrets, am I? Well, I might just have to find out about Tommy."

"Well, that might just be a good idea."

"What about the ranch?"

"Maybe Tommy'll want to join you here."

She sighs. "I might want to...go someplace else."

"Washington?" he asks. When she nods, he says, "There are other ways to be involved, you know—without being there, that is."

"And maybe things there are just fine the way they are."

They look at each other and burst into peals of laughter.

"Okay, maybe not so much," Missy admits.

A few days later, as she's watering the new plants that sit in the new kitchen-window sunshelf Matt built for her, Missy spies Frank pulling into their driveway. As she goes out to greet him and sees his face, though, her smile fades.

"I don't even have to tell you," he says, dabbing at his eyes with a handkerchief. "I can tell by the look on yer face you already know."

"When did she die?"

"This morning. It was so quick—we were practically in the middle of a conversation and...that was it. She was done."

"Oh, Dad." She leads him to one of the porch chairs, sits beside him, and takes his hand.

"Oh, Missy Miss."

They stare out over the fields, watching the horses and cattle graze in their various assigned pastures.

"She didn't tell me what y'all were talking about this past while, since just before yer accident, but whatever it was, it changed her. Made her....freer somehow. She was the happiest in the last few months than I'd ever seen her in her whole life. Even with you having another car wreck and losing the baby and all."

Even with knowing her daughter really died.

"What are you going to do?"

Frank sighs. His oxygen tank makes little sucky noises as he breathes. "I might go stay with Rod in Montana fer a while," he finally says. "After the funeral, that is. We'd been meaning to do that fer years. Didn't know we had a time limit." Tears slip down his face.

Missy kisses his hand as tears slip down her face, too.

As soon as she spies Tommy riding Mystery back from the far fields, Missy wanders out to the stable.

"What's up?"

"What's *up?*"

"That's what I just asked you. Yer supposed to answer before you can ask," he smiles.

"What's *up?*"

"There you go again!"

"Wanna go for another ride?"

"Sure."

He saddles up Harmony while she does the same to Diamond Girl. Before climbing up on her back, she throws her arms around her horse's neck once again.

"Got a hitch in yer giddy up?"

"You beings have the strangest expressions."

"And what kind of beings would that be?"

Uh oh. Oops. "You...Kansas beings."

"More'n just us Kansas beings would say that line. Plus I was just trying to be cute. And I failed miserably because you obviously had no idea what I was saying."

She's starting to really, really enjoy it when her heart flutters.

They ride out to the far edge of the pasture. Andy's house looks abandoned, and she breathes a sigh of relief.

"I kinda helped him with that decision, some," Tommy says.

She looks over at him and takes a big gulp of the crisp air. "Tommy, I'm not from these parts."

"I know."

"What do you mean, you know?"

"I just...know."

"And not just because I made that crack about 'you beings' before?"

"Nope."

Missy looks at him and realizes he really does know. "How long—"

"Since I first saw you after the first accident."

"What the hell? I'm flunking Starbeing 101. Most of us come here and we're never recognized. No one ever figures out that we're not the person we took over."

"Can't help ya. Don't have too much experience with this kinda thing."

"Well, you all have more experience with it than you know."

"Could be."

"How'd you know I wasn't the old Missy?"

"Just knew. Fer one thing, the old Missy wouldn't give me the time of day."

"Was she blind?"

He chuckles at her compliment. "She was...crotchety. Crotchety is not in yer repertoire."

"Could've chalked that up to my supposed amnesia."

"Nah. Completely different energy." He pauses. "Plus, what really gave it away was I overheard you talking to Diamond Girl about it when you first got back."

Missy gasps. Then she nudges his leg with her foot—playfully. "Oh, you!"

"I thought it was just some crazies from yer coma, but then over some time I realized it wasn't so crazy. You were different... and really could've been from someplace else."

"Why didn't you say anything about it?"

"Wasn't up to me." Tommy goes quiet.

"You know, this strong, silent-type thing you have going on is very appealing."

Tommy smiles, his dimples melting her heart yet again.

"I don't mean to sound rude," he says, "but what did you come here for? What did you want to tell us?"

"Can I let you in on a secret? We're all from somewhere else. Most humans do remember it at some point, like when they're dying. Some become aware of it all the time, some start to remember it when they go to sleep at night."

"Yep."

"You knew that, too?

"Yep. We all go home every night. Just a few remember it, though."

Missy raises her eyebrows, impressed at how much this particular human knows. "Earth's such a strange place to be. Every night our souls are set free to wander the universe, and then we make a crash landing back to this place. So much beauty. So much pain. But we all want to come back here, every time. Well, most of us, most of the time."

Tommy nods, not indicating whether he'd never heard these thoughts before or if this was common knowledge to him. She bet it's the latter, which he confirms.

"All of us Zen farmers and ranchers might surprise a few billion people. We have all this time and space on our hands, which give us the opportunity to think about a lot of things. A *lot* of things."

Missy smiles at him.

"What do you look like when yer not here being a human?" he asks.

"Well, that's kind of hard to explain. What I look like depends on who and what is looking at me. Actually, it's kind of like that here, too. But I shapeshift according to my mood. Humans can do that, too, though—some more than others."

Tommy nods again, absorbing that information.

"I'm going to a gathering with other beings like me pretty soon."

"Y'all having some kind of convention or something somewhere?"

"Or something," she smiles.

"What's it like where yer from?"

Missy repeats pretty much what she'd said when Linda asked her the same question, including the comparison of the dark and light of Earth. "You ever think of anything like that?" she asks Tommy.

"Yep."

"You've considered all that before?"

"Yep."

"Are you one of us?"

"Nope."

Missy laughs. "Most people on Earth talk a lot without saying much. You don't talk a lot but every syllable conveys so much."

They ride the horses back to the stable. They remain quiet as they remove the saddles and brush the horses.

"I need to leave Kansas and go do some things."

Tommy doesn't say anything; he just focuses on brushing Harmony.

"There's a lot to learn and do out there," she adds.

"What about the great lesson of truly bein' right where ya are?"

"Well, there's that, too." She hesitates. "Tommy, Matt and I broke up."

"How's that now?" His western-Kansas drawl isn't quite as drawl-like as it usually is—mostly because he says it so quickly to get to hear the answer more quickly.

"We did. He's moving to Denver."

Not wasting another single solitary second, Tommy sweeps her up in his arms, swings her around, and plants a huge kiss on her almost-a-year-long-waiting mouth.

Oh, that kiss! Her head hums as their mouths stay pressed together. The magic of that kiss turns the hum into a buzz as the focus of the entire universe is their mouths and lips and tongues.

And they make love, right there in the freshly set out hay in an empty stall. The horses don't seem to mind, especially since the two humans seem to be enjoying themselves so much.

Ohhhhhhhhh! You crazy humans can't complain about one thing, ever. This is one of the best things in all of creation. Well, this and that car'mul thing.

And the horses still don't seem to mind even when they fall asleep and stay the night.

The first ray of sunshine greets them, although they'd long been awake, making love again.

"Did you know the first ray of sun over the horizon delivers a message?"

"Yep."

"What was yours?"

"Take good care of this woman. Although she doesn't really need any caretaking. And yours?"

"Take good care of this man. Although he doesn't really need any caretaking either. It's just the idea of it."

"Yep."

Later that morning she walks into the house as Matt closes up his suitcase.

"Meanwhile, in this part of," he switches to a television-announcer voice, "*As the Galaxy Turns....*"

She giggles.

"I have to go take care of a few things in Wichita," he says. "But then I'll come back fer yer momma's funeral and leave right after."

"Okay. So I'll say this here then, in case we're sur-rounded by people at the memorial. Thank you for all your love and patience as you eased me into the Earth realm. You're a truly amazing being."

"Takes one to know one. And yer welcome." He pauses in the doorway. "Thank *you*, Ashera."

Tears spring to her eyes. "You're welcome, Matt."

He leaves.

At the memorial, Missy stares at the poster-sized picture of a much younger Linda holding a baby Missy while Rod and Frank stand behind her. Missy thinks back to the last conversation she had with her Earth mother.

"Did you come on a starship?" Linda asked her.

"Kind of. It's all metaphorical. Kind of like life here—it's all metaphorical."

"What one thing would you tell all humans, if you could?" Linda queried.

"That the pain you have to endure on this planet is what makes you so special. It's what can turn you into a superstar." As tears fill Linda's eyes, Missy continues. "That you're among the luckiest beings in all of creation with the amazingly beautiful things you get to experience through your five senses."

Linda brushes her tears away.

"I'd also say, 'Remember humans that you are light and to light you shall return.'"

Welcome back to the light, Momma.

Tommy wanders up to the kitchen door a couple of hours after the memorial.

"Matt leave for Denver?"

"Yes."

"You have any idea how his parents took it?"

She looks at him, trying to gauge how much he knows. "You knew that, too?"

"Yep."

"Did he ever say...?"

"Nope."

"Then why were so you into me 'keeping my agreement,' as you put it?"

"'cause an agreement was still there."

Missy shakes her head at this frustrating human. "He wants to sell you his share of the barn, stables, horses, and cattle."

"'kay."

"You could live in the house."

"Oh, no. I might build another on the other side of the land. We could rent this one out. Plus my farmhouse."

"We?"

"If yer up fer a we."

He watches her face, and as she starts to smile, he does the same. They wander out to the front porch, just in time for the sunset.

"We could sell the cattle, if you want, and do something else."

"I'd love that." She pauses. "Tommy, much as you like the idea of planting yourself in one place and truly being where you're at and all, I do have to go to some places to do some things."

"'kay."

"You want to come with me?"

"Nope. Do whatever it is ya need to do. I'll be waitin' fer ya. Raghtchere."

"Raghtchere is a pretty good place."

"It is."

THANK YOU

To my beautiful husband Steve—my very own Kansas farmboy.

My stepchildren, my late parents, and my siblings.

All the beautiful folks I met in Kansas, especially Alan and Linda, Bobbi, Constance, Deb, Elizabeth, Gerald, Holly, Ian and Lori, Kelly, Marion, Maurine, Pam, Shye and Robert, and Sue and Steve.

My spectacular, special team: Athena McDowell, Barbara Cox, my sister Betsey Crawford, Dana Swift, Eugene Holden, Grace Sears, Jennie Ashanta Lipari, Rev. Karyl Huntley, Kiara Windrider, Laurie Manley, Rev. Lee McNeil Nash, Linda Eisenberg, Lonnie Burkholder, and Veronica Entwistle.

The *Fresh off the Starship* team: Alysa Sanzari-Hall for another beautiful cover; Cheryl Cruts; Frances Mary Frane; Terri Garofalo; and Kathy Meis, Shilah LaCoe, and the other wonderful folks at bublish.com, my distributor.

Jim Self, Roxane Burnett, and the M.A. Players/LLB; Joan and John Walker, Melainah Yee, and the beautiful folks in SD; and Rev. Michael Bernard Beckwith, whose wisdom and love fill this book.

Team VIII of the Veterans Vietnam Restoration Project, especially Bob, Buster, and Daven, whose stories are shared here. Joining this team, making a document-tary of the journey, hearing the stories, and watching these men heal their wounds of war was one of the honors of my lifetime.

The musicians of the playlist for writing this book: Anael, Ben Leinbach and Jai Uttal, Cynthia Snodgrass and Jim Oliver, Darpan and Bhakta, Deva Premal and Miten, Deuter, Erika Luckett and Lisa Ferraro, Karunesh, Krishna Das, Snatam Kaur, Wakela, and Yanni. You are *so* important to this process!

BOOKS BY ANN CRAWFORD

Available on Amazon
in paperback, Kindle, and audiobook versions

Romantic Comedies / Contemporary Fiction

Fresh off the Starship
A romantic comedy about a starbeing who ends
up in the wrong place, right time.

Life in the Hollywood Lane
Quirky, humorous jaunt through an actor's
recovery after her BFF's suicide.

Angels on Overtime
Playful romantic comedy about what happens in
the scenes behind the ones behind the scenes.

Alternative & Fantasy

Spellweaver
Mystical journey with a healer during the
Burning Times.

Mary's Message—
An Alternative History of Mary Magdalene and Jesus
That title pretty much explains it.

Non-fiction

The Life of Your Love
Some suggestions on how to find the love of your life.

*Visioning—Creating the Life of Our Dreams
and a World that Works for Us All*
That title pretty much explains this one, too.

ABOUT THE AUTHOR

Ann Crawford is the author of seven books as well as a screenwriter and an award-winning filmmaker. She has lived "Oh, all over," from one shining sea to the other shining sea to the prairie and then to the mountain. (Yes, we're definitely mixing up our patriotic songs here.) That prairie part includes Kansas for a few years. Right now she and her husband live with a view of Colorado's Rocky Mountains out the window.

You are always welcome to follow Ann's effervescent blog at anncrawford.net as well as visit her on Facebook, Twitter, Instagram, Pinterest, and Amazon.

To inquire about having Ann speak or do a book reading for your group or book club either in person or via Skype, please email info@lightscapespublishing.com.